Master of the Dark Side

Mountain Masters & Dark Haven 4

Ms. Sinclair delivers a deliciously sensual and dark drama that throws the reader into a whirlwind of domination, tenderness and desire that is truly delightful. The author's outstanding talents lie not just in the plotting and pace of the story but in creating the strong, passionate and charismatic characters that run as deep as their sense of honor... Another one for the keeper shelf!

~ The Romance Studio

Real Doms terrify her, so Summer plays with lightweights only. And only in the safety of her club, Dark Haven. But on Western Night, the tough cop who wins her in a sub-roping game is as powerful as they come.

Virgil's first taste of BDSM was disturbingly enticing. Hoping to burn out his interest, he visits an infamous San Francisco club, where he wins himself the prettiest little submissive he's ever seen. He's in a quandary. A man shouldn't render a woman helpless, let alone spank her ass. But the nervous little submissive clearly loves being in his ropes. Her need to be controlled is as powerful as his need to control. So he indulges himself, and her.

That one night could be the beginning, but instead it's the end. She won't play outside the club and he lives too far to visit often. He'll just have to find a way to forget her...or get her in his ropes to stay.

This story wrung me out, pulling me 'every which way' through the full gamut of emotions. I was however, left sated and limp as a cooked wet noodle on the floor... Wow, such a terrific story!

~ Whipped Cream Reviews

Want to be notified of the next release?

Sent only on release day, Cherise's newsletters contain freebies, excerpts, and articles.
Sign up at:
www.CheriseSinclair.com/NewsletterForm

Master of the Dark Side

Mountain Masters & Dark Haven: 4

Cherise Sinclair

VanScoy Publishing Group

Master of the Dark Side

Copyright © 2012 by Cherise Sinclair
Print Edition
ISBN 978-0-9861195-2-1
Published by VanScoy Publishing Group
Cover Artist: Hot Damn Designs
~ Reprint ~

This book previously appeared as a novella in the Doms of Dark Haven anthology. This book is a work of fiction. The names, characters, places, and incidents are products of the writer's imagination or have been used fictitiously and are not to be construed as real. Any resemblance to persons, living or dead, actual events, locales, business establishments, or organizations is entirely coincidental.

Warning: This book contains sexually explicit scenes and adult language and may be considered offensive to some readers. This book is for sale to adults only, as defined by the laws of the country in which you made your purchase.

Disclaimer: Please do not try any new sexual practice, without the guidance of an experienced practitioner. Neither the publisher nor the author will be responsible for any loss, harm, injury, or death resulting from use of the information contained in this book.

Author's Note

To my readers,

The books I write are fiction, not reality, and as in most romantic fiction, the romance is compressed into a very, very short time period.

You, my darlings, live in the real world, and I want you to take a little more time in your relationships. Good Doms don't grow on trees, and there are some strange people out there. So while you're looking for that special Dom, please, be careful.

When you find him, realize he can't read your mind. Yes, frightening as it might be, you're going to have to open up and talk to him. And you listen to him, in return. Share your hopes and fears, what you want from him, what scares you spitless. Okay, he may try to push your boundaries a little—he's a Dom, after all—but you will have your safe word. You will have a safe word, am I clear? Use protection. Have a back-up person. Communicate.

Remember: safe, sane, and consensual.

Know that I'm hoping you find that special, loving person who will understand your needs and hold you close.

And while you're looking or even if you have already found your dearheart, come and hang out with the Mountain Masters.

Love,
Cherise

Chapter One

WELL, IF HE turned out to be a pervert, Dark Haven was sure the right place to come. Virgil Masterson tucked his thumbs under his belt and stared around the huge room. It was Western Night at San Francisco's notorious BDSM club, and the combination of fetishwear and cowboy clothing was mindboggling.

When a tiny brunette submissive walked by wearing nipple clamps, a purple thong, and cowboy boots, he could only shake his head and laugh. Amazing. At least with all the jeans and cowboy shirts, he didn't stand out like a redneck from a small mountain town.

As he listened to the country-western music, he tried to decide on a plan of action. By the end of the night, he intended to know if he was just a normal guy turned on by weird sexual shenanigans or something…worse. He'd always liked being in control in the bedroom—didn't most men?—but then his in-laws had introduced him to a whole new level of control. To BDSM. Stunned the hell out of him.

Under the Hunts' direction, he'd dominated a submissive. Tied her up. She'd melted under his hands, his commands, and climaxed from a hard pinch on her nipples. Damn him for ever getting sucked into this, because now…now when he had sex, he knew exactly what was lacking. He wanted—needed—the extra punch of a woman's willing submission.

As he looked around, he spotted the crowd parting to let a man pass. The dom, dressed in a gambler's rig of striped silk shirt, ornate burgundy vest, and arm garters, walked up and extended his hand. "Virgil Masterson, I believe?"

"That's right." Virgil gave him a cop's assessing once-over: six-two, muscular, around two hundred pounds, black hair in a long braid, black eyes, reddish brown coloring. He took the man's hand, noting the powerful grip. The guy did more with his time than sit around the bar.

"The Hunt brothers asked me to watch for you. I am Xavier, the owner."

Virgil gave an amused snort. As the eldest of three sons, he'd never been subjected to a babysitter...until he stepped into the BDSM scene. "Quite a place."

Xavier acknowledged the compliment with a tilt of his head. "The street level is for dancing, drinking, and watching the shows." He gestured to platforms on either side of the long room, one empty, the other with a domme whipping a slender male sub. "They said you're new to the scene?"

"Yes." Virgil studied the stage performance. He'd used a whip on livestock, never on a human, and the thought didn't appeal to him at all. "I've played at a couple parties and gone on their BDSM camp trip. I'm still..." Frowning, he pushed up the brim of his hat. "I have a problem with the idea of bondage, let alone hurting anyone. I was raised to protect women. Hell, it's my job."

Xavier said mildly, "But if bondage and pain is what the submissive wants? Needs?"

Then he was in trouble. "Guess I'll figure out where I draw the line." That's what he'd come here to do, after all. To observe and investigate in a place well away from Bear Flat. *To figure out if I really am a pervert.*

"If the Hunts worked with you, I assume you know the usual courtesies of observing quietly, not touching another dom's sub or equipment, and the basics of safe, sane, and consensual play."

Virgil nodded.

"Then enjoy your evening. The dungeon is downstairs. If you'd care for an introduction to a submissive, please don't hesitate to ask." Xavier glanced at Virgil's well-worn boots and smiled. "Calf roping starts in a bit—sub roping, in this case. You might find it a good way to meet someone."

Sub roping? He hadn't planned to participate—well, maybe he'd considered it—but damn. "Sounds like fun."

After Xavier left, Virgil checked out the upstairs. A bar was located in one corner, surrounded by tables. The giggling submissive riding a mechanical bull held his attention for a while. Line dancing. A poker game tempted him briefly, but a pretty brunette sub kneeling at one man's feet kept giving her dom concerned glances. Too tense for his mood tonight. *You're not here to play cards, Masterson.*

He took the stairs down to the dungeon. And stopped. At the Serenity Lodge parties, only a handful of scenes occurred at any one time. Dark Haven had...more. His gaze drifted down the long room: several St. Andrew's crosses, stocks, and a whipping post. Sets of chains dangled from a low rafter. Cages, spanking benches, sawhorses, bondage tables. Scene after scene. Throaty moans, high screams, whining, whimpering, and groaning. *Jesus, Mary, and Joseph.* All his cop instincts shouted for him to get his cuffs out and start arresting people.

Yet the dominant in him noted that the scenes were hot as hell. Like the redhead getting wax poured on her nipples. Glazed eyes. Moaning. Her dom had spread her legs to let everyone view her soaked pussy.

At the next scene, a dark-haired domme ran a device like a pizza cutter with tiny metal spikes around a man's nipples. Poor guy had a woody so hard a cat couldn't scratch it.

Unlike the scent of beer, cologne, and perfume upstairs, the dungeon smelled of sweat and leather and so much sex that he could feel testosterone flooding his veins. He stopped at one area to watch a dom with a single-tail delicately lashing a dress from his sub. Fucking fine technique.

Feeling a presence beside him, he looked down to see a pretty little submissive.

"Excuse me," she said, her melodic voice like a meadowlark in a valley of pain.

He stepped back to let her edge past and gave her a slow once-over. *Very nice.*

A leather skirt barely covered her grabbable, round ass. Heeled cowboy boots showcased bare legs, and her full breasts pushed a laced-up leather vest open so far her nipples almost showed. Golden blonde hair, straight and silky, hung to her midback. When she looked back to whisper a thank-you, her eyes were as clear and blue as the sky over the Sierras in June.

Down, boy.

He sighed as the little sub knelt beside the dom. Apparently she wasn't available. Then again, she sure didn't focus on her dom's every movement as if she wanted to serve him with all her being. With the Hunts and some others he'd seen, their dominance over their subs showed up like heat waves in July. And didn't that sound a tad too woo-woo for a cop?

With a snort, and one last regretful look at the sub, Virgil wandered on.

REFUSING TO LISTEN to Mark whine, Summer Aragon dragged him away from the whipping scene to the upstairs stage. The calf roping had started.

Bouncing on her toes, she watched a dom chase after a collared older submissive on the raised platform. Almost to the end, he managed to grab her and toss her down on the well-padded platform. As he tried to bind her ankles and wrists, the crowd roared advice, cheering in yeehaws and whoops and whistles. *God, didn't that look like fun?*

"And another sub bites the dust." Mark slung an arm around her shoulders and pulled her against his lanky frame. "I'm heading home. You gonna come over?"

"Leave now?" After she'd spent all yesterday shopping for just the right leather skirt and vest? She gave him an exasperated stare. When he'd shown up in a T-shirt and jeans instead of western wear, she should have known he'd bow out early. "We haven't been here even an hour."

"Don't care. I had a rough day."

A rough day of programming? *Please.* She thought of her own day as charge nurse for the surgical floor: filling in for the med nurse, transferring a patient to the ICU, wading through reams of doctors' orders, managing a code right at the end of her shift—successful, but God, the paperwork—fixing the diet orders the kitchen had screwed up...and on and on. "Don't you want to join the calf roping?"

"Nah. Jason lent me a new apocalypse movie, and I want to see it."

She considered briefly: a cozy winter evening watching TV or finding someone to play with here. *Play, play, play.* "I'm going to stay a little longer. I've got an urge to be a *calf.*"

"Go for it." He frowned. "I don't think Rick or Mike are here though."

Summer bit her lip. No buddies? That wasn't good.

She only scened with a few doms, ones who were just friends outside the club. Lightweight scenes, lightweight doms. She didn't want more. That would mean dealing with a real dominant—like the darkly tanned man watching the whipping downstairs whose slow scrutiny had heated her from the toes up and set her insides to quivering. *Not for me, thank you.*

But if her buddies weren't here, who would she play with? She glanced up, realized Mark was considering staying...just for her. She smiled at him. "Go home, Mr. Couch Potato."

"That's me." He gave her a relieved look and added, "Sis is having everyone over for Sunday brunch. She said to invite you so you can get your kid fix in."

"I'd love it." She kissed him lightly before he headed for the exit.

A whooping scream pulled her attention to the far corner where a submissive had been thrown off the mechanical bull. Laughing like a loon, the brunette forfeited her bustier and climbed back on. The bull started to buck and twist. Summer winced as the submissive's breasts bounced in conflicting directions.

In another corner, people line danced to Tim McGraw's "I Like It, I Love It." One row held only unattached submissives, both male and female, wearing very few clothes. Tempted to join, she observed for a second. More bouncing breasts—and balls and cocks and butts.

Summer folded her arms over her full chest. Just watching was painful. No, she wanted to be a calf, she really did. But without her safe buddies?

Hmm. Recently she'd thought about testing her nerve by playing with other doms...easy ones, of course. Was this a hint from the gods?

I can do this. Determinedly, she joined the submissive queue, trying to figure out the rules. To her dismay, Xavier and Simon sat at a table by the stage, matching up each dom and calf. They'd make the choice for her? Her stomach clenched. What if she got a sadist?

But Simon was supervising. He'd been all protective since his party last year where Dirk had hurt her so badly, and he'd surely not choose someone cruel. Besides, if the dom caught her, she could still negotiate what the session afterward would involve. And they'd play here in a public place.

Despite her self-assurances, her heart rate increased as she neared the front.

The audience groaned as a sub managed to evade the chasing

dom. The blonde, giggling in a high voice, jumped off the stage. Adjusting her skintight latex dress, she trotted back to the end of the line.

Xavier glanced at the sub in front of Summer and announced, "Jen is next. Gentlemen?"

The contenders raised their hands, and after a moment, Simon pointed to a tall, lanky man. "Aaron. Good luck. She's a fast little critter."

Jen and Aaron took their places.

My turn. Summer stepped up to the desk and waited for the two doms to notice her.

With dark hair and dark eyes, Simon and Xavier appeared like a matched set although Xavier looked flashier in his gambler's clothing. In his forties, Simon was older and attired as an 1860's banker. Rich, classy, powerful doms—so not her kind.

"Summer, it's good to see you." Simon motioned her forward and asked quietly, "How are you doing?"

"I'm fine. Thank you, Sir."

"Are you being careful?"

After she'd healed, he'd given her a lecture on safety measures, and she'd listened carefully. One set of scars from a misjudgment was enough. "Yes, Sir. I never play anywhere but here."

He straightened, a crease forming between his brows. "That's taking prudence a little too far, pet. How can you form a relationship if you won't leave here?"

At the thought of being tied up and alone with a dom—a real dom—she felt as if someone had run a cold hand up her spine. "I'm happy being a sub here."

Xavier frowned also. "A sub? You're not submitting; you only go through the motions. Playacting."

Just team up on me, why don't you? And you're wrong. Her chin went up. "I believe that's up to me." When Xavier's eyes turned to black ice, she gulped out a hasty, "My Liege."

His forefinger tapped the desk for one beat.

She had a vision of being caged and hung from the ceiling like the last sub who'd displeased him.

Another tap.

Or up on the stage being used for flogging practice.

He finally nodded. "That is your choice."

She took a relieved breath. *Thank you, God.*

Xavier turned to the crowd. "Gentlemen, this is Summer. Who would like to win her submission?"

Oh great. Make a big deal of the submission part. Thanks, Xavier. She turned to see an ego-stroking number of hands had gone up. A couple of sadists, some younger doms, and—her gaze was trapped by intent hazel eyes shaded by a black cowboy hat. The rest of the crowd blurred and faded away, leaving only the darkly tanned dominant she'd seen earlier.

He studied her; then his lips curved in a faint smile. He raised his hand to compete.

Her heart gave a nasty thud. *Oh God.*

"Virgil, I believe this little calf is a good one for you. She'll need a steady hand," Xavier said.

As if she were caught in a dream, she watched the dom— Virgil—move forward through the crowd. He looked appallingly big. A couple of inches over six feet. Dirk's height. Probably about as heavy too, but this dom was as solid as the mechanical bull. He wore a scuffed black hat, faded cowboy shirt, and well-worn boots; she doubted his western outfit was a costume.

As he stopped beside her, his level, assessing eyes met hers, and the floor seemed to shiver like quicksand under her feet.

He glanced at Xavier. "Thank you." He sounded pleased, thank God, since she really didn't want to annoy him. Why did he have to be as big as Dirk? He made her feel like a little calf, and she glanced down to make sure she hadn't grown hooves.

The sun lines beside his eyes crinkled. When he took her hand, hard calluses on his fingers scraped her palm. "Nice to meet you, Summer." His rough baritone voice curled around her in a dark embrace.

All the spit in her mouth dried up, yet she wanted to move closer. *Confused much, Summer?*

"Are you ready to play?" Virgil asked, unsnapping his shirt cuffs and shoving his sleeves up to his elbows.

Lord have mercy. Even his heavy-boned wrists were muscular. *But he's not Dirk, and I'm going to be a calf.* Her excitement started to rekindle. *An ornery calf.* "Only if you catch me."

His growling laugh almost made her knees buckle.

"I'm glad to see you here, Virgil," Simon said and added, "By the way, this little sub had a bad experience last year, but it's time for her to move past it."

Summer's jaw dropped. "You... Damn you, that's none of your busi—"

A hand covered her mouth completely, and a voice rumbled in her ear, "I'm new to the club, but I'd say that disrespecting a dom is a piss-poor idea."

Oh hell. Xavier came down hard on rudeness.

Seeing the cold stare he gave her, she tried to back away, except Virgil's unmovable, rock-hard body pressed right up against hers. Xavier turned his gaze to Virgil. "Are you still interested?"

"Definitely."

"She will need to be reprimanded for her rude behavior."

Virgil didn't speak for a long moment, then said, "I understand."

"Very good." Xavier tilted his head toward the stage. "You're up."

Summer climbed the steps, way too conscious of the big dom behind her. He'd punish her? The thought of his strong hand coming down on her bottom—of having a real spanking—sent anticipation zinging through her. She glanced over her shoulder.

Such a serious expression, brows together, mouth in a tight line. But as he watched the stage where Aaron had just tossed Jen over his shoulder, laughter appeared in his eyes.

Summer smiled. He had a sense of humor after all. *Oh, this might be totally great.*

On the platform, the male sub directing the roping pointed to a big sack. "Boots and shirt go in there, Sir." He checked her. "Your boots too."

She got one boot off, but then Virgil removed his shirt and, oh Lord, her gaze got stuck on the impressive contours of his chest. With every movement, muscles rippled under his tanned skin. As he pulled his boots off, his biceps bunched, making her fingers tingle with the need to touch and discover if his muscles were as hard as they looked.

He caught her staring and smiled—not a conceited I-work-out-and-have-a-great-body type smirk, but more of a I'm-a-boy; you're-a-girl; life-is-good. He nodded at her remaining boot.

Oh, right. She yanked it off.

"Okay, Sir and sub." The sub handed Virgil two pieces of short rope from a box and pointed to a taped line ten feet away. "When she reaches the yellow line, you give chase. If she gets to the far side or you can't restrain her within the time limit, you lose. No tackling."

"Got it." Virgil gave her a slow smile. "I don't think she's that fast."

She eyed him as he put the ropes between his teeth. God, this was too fun. Her competitive spirit ordered, *Run like hell.* Her inner submissive said, *Let him catch me.* The gung ho voice won, and she leaned forward.

The sub yelled, "Go!"

Chapter Two

F EET SLAPPING ON the plastic padding, Summer tore across the stage as fast as she could. She passed the yellow line.

She heard him behind her, the sound of his heavy stride drowning hers out. Closer. Several feet before the end, he grabbed her arm, spinning her around him until she faced the wrong way.

She staggered, tried to regain her balance, and he moved on her like a massive bear. She squeaked and backpedaled.

Grinning, he swung his foot behind her right ankle and tripped her. With a yelp, she fell backward. Her hat went flying.

He caught her on the way down, his hand gently cradling her head as he dropped to one knee beside her. Before her brain had stopped spinning, he'd rolled her onto her stomach.

No surrender. She shoved up.

His knee on her butt pinned her to the mat. Despite her flailing and kicking and giggling uncontrollably, he caught one ankle, then the other, and tied them together.

When he reached for her left wrist, she yanked it away, holding her hands above her head and out of his reach. If she used up enough time, he'd lose.

"Stubborn little calf." His deep laugh sent quivers through her. As he slid his knee up to her midback so he could reach her wrists, his weight squished her breasts painfully against the padding. After grabbing her arms, he moved off and far too easily secured her hands behind her back.

She tugged on the ropes, feeling no give. She couldn't break free. No escape. *No escape...* Her breath hitched. Twisting her head, she stared up at him, and his size kept growing until he seemed huge—bigger than Dirk. Nightmarish memories bound her tighter than the ropes. *Tied. Trapped. Agony. Screaming.*

She whimpered.

"Whoa, sweetie." He lifted her to her knees and cupped her chin in his palm. His eyes were steady, not angry, not filled with lust. "You're all right, Summer." His rough croon, like a gravel road under soft tires, flattened out her fears.

She inhaled slowly. *Idiot. This isn't Dirk. I'm on a stage.* Couldn't get much more public or safer than that. "Sorry," she whispered.

He chuckled. "You're not the first calf I've terrorized in my time." He raised his hands in the air—a rodeo gesture—and, as the audience cheered loudly, pulled her to her feet. He hadn't even lost his hat.

She huffed a laugh; she hadn't had a chance against him. Still feeling a little off-balance, she asked, "You did rodeo?"

"In my wayward youth. I never caught such a pretty calf before, though." His lazy grin turned her insides topsy-turvy—even before he tossed her over his shoulder.

All the blood rushed to her head. A sub scooped up her hat, carefully set it in with the boots, and handed the sack to Virgil.

"Thanks." Virgil stepped off the stage and sauntered across the room, giving Summer a dizzying upside-down view of the crowd: the receptionist, Destiny, almost naked except for plastic six-shooters. A dom with a lariat on his hip, his stalking gait that of a predator hunting a stray calf.

When Virgil turned, boots, purple suspenders, a leather thong, a chest harness, and a red velvet gown spun around her. She blinked and focused on something closer—the thick, flexing muscles on each side of his spine, the tight fit of his faded jeans over his flat butt.

When he massaged the back of her thigh with a calloused hand, heat streamed through her. She'd carefully stayed away from big men all this year, and now her hormones apparently wanted to make up for lost time.

As Virgil carried her down the stairs to the dungeon, the sounds of sex and pain smothered the country-western music from above. They passed the punishment room, where a dom was using a belt on a strapped-down sub who wore only white chaps.

A tremor ran through Summer. What did Virgil plan to do for her punishment?

He walked halfway through the room, then set her on her feet in front of a chair and steadied her. "Kneel here, please. I want to talk with you before we do anything." He gripped her upper arms and lowered her until her bottom rested on her feet.

As he took a seat in the leather chair, she glanced around. The nearby spanking bench held a sub, restrained and gagged. *Gagged.* Unable to scream, to yell her safe word, to beg her dom to stop. *God.* The memory of being in that situation chilled her bones. "Untie me."

He had a hard face, all bone and muscle with a strong jaw, and the slow smile he gave her didn't transform his appearance into a nice, easy-going man. With his fingertips, he lifted her chin. "Now, Summer, I'm pretty new to BDSM, but even I know you don't talk to a dom in such a manner."

New to BDSM? And he made her head spin just from the power in his gaze? His hand held her face tilted up to him, so she couldn't look away. "I'm sorry," she muttered. She noticed with a thrill of anxiety—and excitement—that his shoulders were as wide as the chair back.

"Almost adequate. You can call me Virgil." His fingers loosened as he rubbed his thumb over her lower lip. A glint of humor appeared in his eyes, and his lips quirked. "I don't like the term *Master*, but I'm used to being called Sir."

His straight-shouldered posture and easy authority did remind her of military men. "Yes, Sir," she said. She regarded him for a minute. A tiny, pale scar showed on one cheekbone, another on his chin, making him appear a little battered, and somehow she liked that. His thick eyelashes were darker than his sandy brown hair and the same color as the beard stubble along his jawline. Reassuring smile lines creased the corners of his eyes and bracketed his mouth.

He released her and rested his thickly muscled forearms on his thighs as he studied her face. "Now tell me what you like and don't like, Summer."

Negotiations. She breathed out in relief. "I won't be gagged. No drawing blood or hard-core pain. No anal." She eyed him and decided on extra caution. "No bondage."

When she'd been ten, she'd had a solo in the school play. The spotlight would track her, focus on her, much like his intent gaze did now. One corner of his mouth turned up, and he ran a finger down her cheek. "Now, I don't particularly like gags. I enjoy the noises a woman makes. We agree on that one. I object to seeing blood or making welts or anything that won't disappear before the next day. We agree there."

Something in her relaxed a bit...until he added, "I do like anal play. Is your limit just for my cock buried in your asshole or for everything?"

Like his fingers? Or toys? She actually squirmed and saw him smile. "Um. For anything large?" Her gaze dropped to his crotch, where something very, very large bulged his jeans.

His laugh held a deep rumble. "I'll take that as a compliment, little sub." He toyed with her tiny spur earring, then stroked his finger across her shoulder, in the hollow above her collarbone, sensitizing her skin. "As for bondage, seems to me as if you're already in restraints."

Her jaw dropped. "Uh...that was to play the roping game."

"Then I'd say it's not a very hard limit. Simon said you'd had a bad experience. Anything to do with being tied up?"

Damn Simon. "No. Yes." She scowled. "It's got nothing to do with our scene." Because the session would occur here in the club, in public. Her muscles relaxed.

"It's odd, but I like seeing you in my ropes." His mouth curved, and his fingers touched her neck, rested on her thudding pulse. "And I get the impression you like being in them, sweetheart. Don't you?"

"But…" What could she say? He was right. Being tied up excited her. A lot. And worried her. A lot. "Yes. I guess."

"Then why don't we see how it goes with you in restraints."

Simon's warning had practically guaranteed Virgil would push her, dammit. But he was exerting only a slight amount of pressure…because he could tell she wanted the bondage. And she did. Somehow, she knew he'd be careful. God, she'd gone insane. "Yes, Sir."

"Good. What's your safe word?"

"It's *safe word*." She'd chosen something anyone involved in BDSM would recognize as a call for help. One more paranoia left over from before.

"Use it if that fear of yours gets to be too much. What about pain?"

How far could she trust him? "I don't like severe pain."

His fingers stroking her neck paused. "Then you're saying you enjoy some."

Those rugged, powerful hands. What would they feel like on her? Hurting her, pushing her, comforting her. She nodded.

He made a noise as if she'd hit him. "All right." His eyes focused on the nearby scene, and he muttered, "Fucking-A," under his breath.

From the sounds of slaps, sobs, and moans, the sub was getting off from the spanking.

His gaze came back to her. "I didn't hear any limit on sex. Or toys."

She felt herself flush. She didn't usually want more than a little domination and a spanking or hand-induced sex. Yet the thought of this…stranger…holding her down and pushing inside her sparked every nerve in her body.

"I…" Why did he have to keep asking for clarifications? Her buddies simply accepted her limits without studying her reactions or questioning her answers. She shifted uncomfortably.

"I know you're not completely at ease. That's good to a degree." He leaned down and dragged her completely between his legs. His thighs closed on her upper arms like iron bars. When he threaded a hand into her long hair and tugged her head back, she stared up at him helplessly, knowing the quivers in her stomach had more to do with anticipation than fear.

"Oh, you're excited, all right. I can see it," he murmured. He tossed his hat on the sack of clothing, and his mouth gently settled on hers. He tasted of mint. Clean and heady. His firm hand curved under her chin as he teased and nibbled at her lips.

With her hands tied behind her back, head trapped by his grip on her hair, and his fingers on her jaw, she couldn't fight his assault—didn't want to fight as heat flooded her veins. Her lips softened, opened.

"That's right. Let me in." He took her mouth hard this time, as forceful as a Midwestern twister, rocking her to the foundation.

When he sat back, she wanted to follow him, to crawl into his lap, to feel his hands on her. The way his knees tightened on her shoulders, pinning her in place, showed he knew…and wouldn't relinquish control and let her.

The knowledge finished off what his kiss had started. She felt the wetness where her bottom pressed against her legs. Her body was screaming, *Yes, yes, yes. Sex!*

He rested a hand on her shoulder, heavy and warm, and she couldn't help but remember the sure strength of his hands as he'd tied her wrists. "Well, sex does seem like a good possibility, doesn't it?" he said in a low tone, watching her with those careful eyes.

Odd hazel eyes. Upstairs in the brighter lights, she'd thought they were green. Here, in the dimmer lighting, they appeared slightly lighter than his tanned skin—a brown with mesmerizing golden flecks. And filled with an intimidating self-possession.

"VIRGIL, COULD I interrupt?"

Virgil looked up from the pretty little sub to see the Hunt brothers' friend, Simon. They'd talked before at one of the Hunts' parties.

"Xavier mentioned you'd come in with no gear," Simon said.

"I hadn't planned to play tonight." Hell, he hoped he'd walk in, get disgusted, and be done with this problem. Instead he'd had the opposite reaction. So now he had a submissive uncomfortable with bondage—only he could see she wanted it—and who definitely enjoyed pain. How could he possibly give her what she needed?

"About what I thought." The dom dropped a leather bag beside Virgil's chair. "When Jake and Logan mentioned your visit, I gathered a sampling of things you might enjoy. Nothing extreme."

"Thanks, Simon, but—"

"Keep it and put them all to good use." His gaze flicked over Summer, and he smiled. "You can start on this impertinent submissive."

The noise she made sounded like the growl his cousin's coon cat would make, and without looking, Virgil set his hand on top of her head. She quieted, and satisfaction washed through him. They were in tune already, and the way she focused on him, looking at him in a way she hadn't with the other dom, gave him a charge almost like an adrenaline rush. "In that case, I accept."

"Excellent. I'm on dungeon monitor duty, so I'll be around." Simon strolled away.

With friends like him, who needs enemies? Virgil frowned at the bag, undoubtedly full of everything needed to render a woman helpless, to keep her restrained. His head said no.

Yet Summer was beautiful, on her knees, bound in his ropes. The desire to please him, to be under his control, showed in her eyes, and something inside him answered to her need.

He nudged his foot against the bag. Undoubtedly it contained equipment to hurt her too. His gut clenched. *But look at her.* Lips parted, cheeks flushed. She'd requested pain, and her wide eyes begged for him to continue.

His cock rose in full agreement, and he sighed. Damned if his dick and a willing sub hadn't outvoted him.

He needed to do this, needed to discover his own limits and try to resolve the conflict. And in the process, he'd damn well be a good dom to her. He rose. "Discussion's over. We've got an available spanking bench right there."

She bit her lip, yet her squirm of anticipation lightened his heart.

He undid the ropes from her wrists and checked the skin. Slightly reddened but no abrasions. He'd taken care when roping her. She had such pretty, smooth skin, and he hadn't done a tie-down of a calf in a while.

After slinging the bag over his shoulder to rest across his back, he lifted her into his arms. Round and soft. He rubbed his chin over her silky hair, breathing the scent in: peaches and vanilla. She smelled edible. Lickable. Fuckable.

Built like a prayer bench, the spanking bench had a padded place to kneel and a higher padded four-by-four for the submissive to bend over. He hadn't used one before, but he'd watched the previous couple. Straightforward enough. Seemed like the proper equipment, since he planned to warm Summer's round ass as part of Xavier's punishment.

A little hurt with no lasting harm. But what if he liked it? Dammit.

He set her down beside the bench, holding her upper arms to help her balance. Although she was average height, she seemed small. Womanly. He smoothed his palms over her curvy body, learning her shape and feel. Her bones were pleasingly padded, her waist curved in nicely, and her full hips begged for the grip of a man's hands.

"Stay right there and don't move." When he reinforced the command with the stern expression he used to intimidate drunks, a tiny shiver ran through her body. *Ah*. Logan had said a dom could often spot a submissive by her reaction to a command. Nice.

She wanted his control—he'd give her what she needed.

Keeping a hand curved around her calf so she wouldn't lose the sense of being restrained, he knelt and opened the bag. Leather cuffs. *Yes*. A telescoping spreader bar. *Oh yeah*. A paddle? His stomach tightened. Then he nodded. *Yes*. Anal toys—*not yet*. The leather belt—hell no.

In fact, part of him insisted he shouldn't use any of this stuff.

But the little sub's arousal hung in the air, a soft fragrance that made him want to hear her whimper and beg for release. He wanted to know everything—her desires, what made her tick. Her voice had caught his attention; her appearance had roused him. Her giggling... Damn, he'd loved that, but the way she'd faced her fears? How could a man resist that combination of submission and courage?

How would she react to the paddle? To his hands? He'd find out how they'd both react. That was why he was here.

She stood quietly as he studied her. He'd scened with some subs at Serenity Lodge, but tonight felt different. He'd take her surrender, yes. He expected to have her squirming under him...but more. This time, he wanted to know the sub. This one. *Summer*.

And to find out about the bad experience Simon had mentioned. Should he have pushed her more? Just how much did restraints really bother her? He'd have to watch her reactions like a hawk.

But right now, the flush in her cheeks and the added pinkness of her lips said she wanted what he had to give. He slid his palm up her thigh to below her pussy, feeling the juices creeping down her leg and the heat of her skin. He left his hand there, enjoying the tiny squirms she gave.

A squirmy soft woman with big blue eyes. He was a dead man.

Chapter Three

WHEN VIRGIL REMOVED the rope ties from her ankles, Summer felt more in control. Less nervous. *Less excited.* But she didn't mind. Being unbound was so much safer and—

Something closed around her left ankle. Her gaze shot down. A cuff? He set a spreader bar next to her feet. She stepped back.

"For each time you move, I'm adding an extra swat."

She closed her eyes at the arousing threat. She'd gone past damp and well into really wet. If he kept talking to her in that rough, sexy baritone, she'd never last.

He cuffed her right ankle. "Open your legs."

She moved her legs apart, and he slapped her inner thighs lightly to make her spread more. God, the tiniest of stings and she almost moaned. Cool air wafted against the wetness of her folds.

As he adjusted the spreader bar, she listened to the sounds around them: the faint beat of country music. A man's low moan. A woman's intermittent shrieks of pain. Low instructions from a dom. A woman's scream of climax. *What would it be like to be so lost in an orgasm as to scream?*

Virgil had made the spreader bar wider than her shoulders. He attached her ankle cuffs to each end. This time when she tried to draw her legs together, she couldn't. The bar held her ankles apart, keeping her exposed. *Oh Lord.*

Still kneeling, he ran his calloused hands up her thighs.

Her breath stopped as his fingers approached her pussy. Her clit throbbed. She needed to be touched right there. Instead he folded her short leather skirt up and tucked the hem into the waist, and did the same in the front. After undoing the bows of her thong, he pulled it off. When he held the scrap of material to his face and inhaled, her cheeks flared with heat.

"You smell nice, like sunshine and sex." His hand cupped her exposed pussy, and he gave a pleased *mmm*. "All shaved and bare—nothing in the way of my tongue."

She hadn't realized she could grow wetter.

He rose, filling space with his solid presence, as if the world might bump into him and he'd never give ground. "Let's get your vest off also. In fact, why don't you undo it for me?"

"Me?" She added quickly, "Yes, Sir."

He stood, feet braced, arms folded over his bare chest, and waited as she fumbled with the leather strings. Finally she reached the last one, and her vest fell open.

"You, honey, have gorgeous breasts." He slid the garment off and cupped her full breasts with hands so large she fit without overflowing. His movements as unhurried as his speech, he weighed and molded them.

When his thumbs circled her bunched nipples, streaks of need shot straight to her clit. Seeing the heat and command in his eyes, she felt as if she'd gone wading and stepped off into deep water. She looked down only to see his muscular forearms and corded wrists and the erotic sight of his tanned hands on her pale skin.

"Eyes on me, sweetheart." He put his fingers under her chin and lifted her face up, holding her there as his other hand rolled her nipple. As he pinched it to the edge of pain, then stroked the ache away, he watched her with a penetrating gaze that pierced all the way to her soul.

When finally he stepped back, heat simmered beneath her skin as if she had a sauna inside her...and the thermostat had broken.

"I saw you with someone earlier, you know. You didn't look

like your head was in the game at all." His eyebrows lifted. "Was it?"

Her breasts were swollen, her nipples burned, and she needed a moment to process his meaning. Then she winced, remembering how Xavier had said she playacted submission. "Uh. I guess not." Xavier was right, darn him. Her buddies never affected her like this, never shook her confidence, never took the control from her hands. They never made her feel sexy.

Under the warm heat in Virgil's eyes, she felt...beautiful.

He pulled more cuffs from the toy bag. "Give me your wrist, Summer."

A tremor ran through her, shaking her balance. Unable to even step back, she chewed on her lip, wanting to protest that she'd already said no to bondage.

His gaze was level. Steady.

She put her hand in his palm. As he fastened the cool leather snugly around one wrist, then the other, the shaking grew inside, not from fear, but from need.

He ran a finger under each cuff and tested the fit. "Use your safe word if you get scared, honey."

"I'm fine." Her voice came out husky.

"Yes, you are, aren't you?" He kissed her lips lightly, then took a seat on the spanking bench. His firm gaze met hers. "I want those breasts," he said softly. "Bring them to me, please."

Her nipples contracted so hard and tight she wanted to whimper with arousal. But she didn't move, because if she did—if she followed his order—then she gave him even more than he'd taken.

His voice turned dangerously low. "Now, Summer."

Her feet shuffled forward without any intention on her part, and under his authoritative gaze, her hands lifted her breasts, offered them to him.

"That's very nice, sweetheart." He set one hand on her bottom, and his other pressed over where her left palm cupped her breast. His warm breath touched her nipple. One breath and another. With the subtle stimulation, her head spun, dizzy with need.

The touch of his warm lips on the peak made her jump.

The grip on her butt tightened, holding her firmly as his tongue circled her nipple. "Mmmm." His deep voice was rich with satisfaction.

When he glanced at her, she tried to back away. "No, Summer. Don't move." He paused. "Why don't you want me to enjoy your breasts?"

No one had ever questioned her so persistently. "Uh." If she said, *I want you to*, he wouldn't believe her, since she'd tried to retreat. If she said, *I don't like it*, he wouldn't believe her, since a blind man could see the way she responded to him. This man was as far from blind as any dom she'd ever met.

"Summer?" His quiet voice ripped her anchoring away like the current in a fast river.

"I...I'm used to a dom taking what he wants. Offering feels different."

"I see. Sweetheart, you're going to offer me a lot more than just your breasts tonight." His baritone was measured and sure.

Her air hissed out at the dark promise in his eyes.

He lowered his head, his lips enclosing her nipple with heat. He sucked hard and fast, and she gave a tiny scream. Each strong pull of his mouth on her breast somehow squeezed her clit too.

When he straightened, she lowered her hands. "Do not move, baby," he growled, and she froze, then pushed her breasts back upward.

"Very obedient. Good girl." His compliment made her float with pleasure.

He touched her between the legs, where her pussy had waited forever for just that. Even so, she jerked at the jolt of exquisite sensation and got a low, "Uh, uh. Stay still, honey." He traced a finger between her labia, slicking the wetness up and over her clit and back down.

Her eyes closed at the incredible pleasure. Her nipples, wet and swollen from his mouth, bunched tightly and throbbed, and his finger multiplied the sensations streaming through her. When he pushed a slick finger up into her, her knees wobbled. *More.*

She opened her eyes to see him watching her with a narrowed gaze.

A flutter started in her stomach. "I—"

"Shhh." With his finger deep inside her, he rubbed his thumb over her clit, making little circles on one side until the nub hardened. Then he switched to the other side. The pressure in her groin grew, and his thick finger in her curled, rubbing something—somewhere—and the electrifying friction unraveled her thoughts completely.

He moved away, leaving her close to the edge. Hurting with need. "You're a beautiful submissive, Summer. I like the way you respond." With sure hands, he lifted her onto the spanking bench and clipped her cuffs behind her back.

She stiffened. "No. No, I don't want my hands restrained."

"Yes. You do." He squeezed her shoulders, massaging the rigidity away. "Bondage scares you for some reason, but you do want it. Need it. That's clear, even to me."

Even to him? She shut her eyes in frustration. He read her more easily than almost anyone in the place.

"Breathe for me, Summer." She sucked in air. He stroked his hands up and down her arms as she tugged at the cuffs, reassuring her with his touch, letting her relax into his dominance. It had been so long since she could let go, could trust someone to have control. "Okay now?" he asked gently.

"Yes, Sir." He'd acknowledged her fears but didn't yield at all. Why did his decisiveness make her feel safer with him than with someone who'd give in to her demands?

He pulled something from the toy bag. "Let's drive you a little crazier, since Simon was so generous." He stepped in front of the spanking bench, amusement lightening the heat in his eyes. He opened a package of nipple clamps. "I assume you've worn these before?"

Oh God, as aroused as she felt, could she take more? Each beat of her heart sent a pulse of blood to her clit.

"Summer?"

"Yes, Sir," she whispered.

"I've learned I like the way a woman's breasts look with this kind of jewelry." With gentle tugs, he shaped her nipple long and taut, fastened on a clamp, and tightened the small screw to the point of pain. She stiffened, staring up in his face.

A muscle flexed in his jaw. "You can take more." And he advanced it a tiny bit further.

She whimpered and tensed.

"Breathe, Summer. Breathe until the pain eases up."

She knew how, but without that low commanding voice caressing her, she might not have managed. A few seconds and the bite of the clamp dulled to a throb matching the one in her pussy.

"Good girl. Now this one."

Uhhh, two make the pain so much worse. Needing to push him away, rip the clamps off, she jerked at her arms—uselessly. The river of awareness that she could do nothing flooded her, sweeping away her willpower. "Virgil, please...no."

His hand stroked her hair. "Breathe again for me, baby. Deep breath now. That's a girl." He had a line between his brows and his mouth had tightened, but his eyes were level on hers.

The burn eased, and God, she needed to come so badly she shook. She squirmed.

"Be damned. You do like some pain, don't you." He wasn't asking but stating a fact. He touched her cheek. "Bend over now."

From kneeling upright, she leaned forward. He adjusted her so her ribs rested on the leather of the four-by-four, and her heavy breasts dangled on the other side. The clamps tugged on her nipples like someone's sharp teeth. And each bite seared straight to her clit.

He sighed, his hand stroking her hair gently. "The pain makes you hotter, doesn't it?"

"Yes, Sir," she said with difficulty. The unstoppable fog of sensation was rolling right over her thoughts.

"Why the hell does watching you take the pain make me hot too?" he muttered. He pulled a wooden paddle from the bag and moved behind her. "I'd make you count, but I'm simply going to continue until I think we're both ready to quit, so there's no point, is there?"

Oh. My. God. She'd never been this needy before. Everything inside her shook. The way he treated her, watched her, commanded her, seemed to pull at something deep in her pelvis, an invisible leash of control. No wonder Xavier had said she'd been playacting.

He kneaded her bottom, and his abrasive palms sent goose bumps up her skin. "You have a gorgeous ass, baby. Soft and round." When his fingers slid between her legs, up and over her clit, as if to remind her of how aroused she was, she groaned. And groaned again when he took his hand away.

Something cool and solid rubbed the skin on her ass. The paddle. He gave her several tiny painless pats like a baby hammering on the floor.

What kind of a spanking was that? Disappointment cooling her excitement, she glanced over her shoulder at him.

The muscles in his face were rigid, his jaw set. The cords stood out on the hand gripping the paddle. His erection was very obvious. He saw her looking. His gaze moved over her slowly, and then a corner of his lip turned up. "All right, baby."

He hesitated for a long moment and swung. No baby pat this time; it stung...stung so good. She moaned as the shock blew straight into pleasure. She lowered her head and gave a happy moan.

He grunted as if he'd been the one to get hit, and then settled in. Slowly the blows grew harder. The pressure in her lower half tightened as the stinging changed to burning, and she edged closer to coming.

He stopped to rub his palm over her bottom, soothing the pain. His finger slid between her folds. "You're wet, Summer." He cupped her chin and turned her head toward him. "And in need of more," he said slowly, and his thumb stroked along her jaw. His eyes darkened. "All right, then."

He released her and stepped back. "These are for being rude to Simon and Xavier." The next five were hard enough to bring tears to her eyes. Each jerk of her body made her breasts swing and the clamps bite, sending more sensation streaming through her body.

Her head spun as her surroundings faded.

All her weight leaned on the bench. Nothing mattered anymore except the next slap of the paddle, the burning between her legs, the tugging on her nipples. Sensation after sensation.

He paused and ran his fingers between her folds, turning slick with her wetness. "Fuck, you really love this. I've never seen anything so beautiful," he said just loud enough for her to hear. His slow stroking over her clit increased the fire until the whole area felt like one exquisitely exposed nerve.

When he moved his hand, she groaned. She'd been so close.

He returned to swatting her, light, then hard, from no pain to slaps that sounded horrible and resounded through her body. Between blows, the clamps teased her throbbing nipples, shooting electricity in a constant stream to her pussy.

Closer. *Hit me. Touch me...* Her back arched, and her butt pushed up, waiting...

He stopped—the bastard stopped. He squeezed her bottom, making her squeak as the burn increased. With his other hand, he stroked her pussy, the sure touches turning her clit back to a throbbing hardness.

"Please," she whimpered, hips wiggling uncontrollably. She wanted to put her thighs together, to rub herself, to do something, but her legs were restrained apart, her hands secured. She could do nothing. "*More.*"

"You'll get more...but it'll be my way, not yours." He resumed spanking her. Each blow forceful, one cheek, the other, and one against the lower curve of her butt. Pain ripped into raw sensation with every slap, first the shock, then the burning, then a wave of pleasure. Her hips rocked back after each as if to beg for more. The humming pulse in her ears grew louder than her moans.

He moved his position forward a step. His free hand brushed down her stomach to settle over her pussy, so that each time he hit her bottom, his finger rubbed directly over her clit.

She keened, her body turning rigid as the pressure inside sky-rocketed upward, coiling…

He swatted her ass mercilessly, and the burning pain mingled with the excruciating pleasure of his finger sliding down the side of her clit. Another cruel slap of the wooden paddle. His finger stopped.

"Oh God, oh God, oh God."

The next swat didn't come…didn't come…and then he stroked ever so slowly over the very top of her clit. Her muscles tensed as everything coiled inside.

The paddle struck.

Pain ripped into her; his finger pressed down on the nub of nerves, and it felt as if a tightly wound ball in her groin exploded. Her insides spasmed, sending sensations blazing through her in fiery bursts of pleasure. Her spine arched. His hands closed on her hips, restraining her, as she bucked in place.

He abandoned her clit to press two fingers over her entrance, then thrust them inside her, hard and fast.

The shock sent her over again. "Nooooo."

He laughed, caressing her stinging bottom. "Oh yes, Summer. God, look at you." His jeans rubbed against her leg, the pressure of his thighs comforting as she shook in his grasp. Sweat covered her body, and her heart hammered hard enough to break through her ribs.

"The way you got off…" He stroked her for a minute, letting her catch her breath, murmuring quiet compliments about the pleasure she'd given him, about sharing her response with him.

His words reassured her. Why did an orgasm make her feel as if she'd opened herself to someone she didn't know? But she didn't know him, did she? The surge of affection, of need for him to hold her, was false, not true at all.

Emotions twisting, she pulled on the restraints, needing to get free, to get up. To get gone. Only, he'd want his turn now, and…

"Shhh." To her surprise, he took her face between his big hands and kissed her, not hungrily as she expected, but sweetly, his lips firm, sure, enticing her to want more. "Thank you, sweetheart."

She sighed when he let her go, and somehow the aching, fearful sensation had eased.

"Better," he murmured. "Now hold on, baby. I've seen what clamps do." He stepped in front of the bench and removed the clamp from her left breast.

Blood rushed into her nipple, bringing a searing whip of pain. She gasped, pulling back from him.

"One more." He took the other clamp off, and God, it burned and hurt. Tears filled her eyes, and she jerked frantically at the restraints holding her arms behind her back.

"Easy, Summer." He unclipped her wrists, and then detached the spreader bar, leaving all the cuffs on.

She held her fingers against her breasts as the fiery pain lessened. How'd she manage to forget how much worse clamps felt coming off than going on?

After a minute or two, a tolerable throbbing replaced the burning. She sighed and realized he stood nearby, keeping an eye on her. Okay, time to play fair. She glanced at his jeans and the very large bulge in front. "Perhaps I can do something in return?"

"Maybe later." He pulled a soft, thin blanket from the toy bag and wrapped it around her. "Let me clean up a bit. I'm sure they have cleaning supplies."

"I can help." To her surprise, her legs wobbled. Then again, she'd never come so hard before. Taking a minute to get stable, she looked around. Near the center of the room, Simon and Xavier talked quietly and watched the scenes. Xavier's dark gaze met hers, and a faint smile appeared on his hard face.

Had he set her up with Virgil deliberately?

Unsettled, she secured her blanket, got the spray bottle and paper towels and wiped down the equipment while Virgil put everything away.

Might as well get dressed, she thought, and found her clothes. When she started to unfasten the blanket, he gave a deep laugh. "Not so fast, blondie." He set the clothing in her hands and scooped her up, making her head spin.

"Put me down."

"Nope." He held her snuggled to his bare chest, tipping her up so he could rub his cheek against hers. "I like carrying you."

He had a clean, crisp masculine scent with hints of soap and an outdoorsy aftershave. Unable to resist, she ran her fingers through his sandy-colored hair. A conservative, short cut—why was she not surprised? Soft, thick, and straight, like the fur on Mark's Siberian husky, and much more fun to play with. His cheek creased as if he enjoyed her hands on him.

She liked them there too.

He found an isolated spot, dropped the toy bag beside the chair, and tossed her clothes on it, then sat down.

Her tender bottom hit his hard thighs, and she winced. When he settled her on his lap rather than having her kneel, she tensed. She only sat on laps for spankings. "Sir, please, I don't want a spanking."

"Good," he said easily. "I think I'm done beating on your ass for tonight…unless you annoy me." His brows drew together. "First you figure I want sex, then that I'll spank you. Summer, don't you ever *talk* to your doms after a scene?"

"Uh. Not a lot."

"Whose fault that you don't?" He didn't sound as if he were blaming her…or the men. Just curious.

"Well, it's not like I get all emotional or anything. I usually leave afterward."

"So your doms don't have the chance." He remained silent for a minute. "One of the nicer things with this BDSM business is the way it forces—or should force—people to talk. I never realized how much I assumed about a partner's perceptions until I started to ask questions. So we're gonna have a chat now, baby."

She stared at him. He wasn't joking. She'd seen couples sitting around after scenes but figured the subs had felt needy. "I'm not upset. I mean, we don't have to talk."

"Yeah, we do." He rubbed his thick knuckles over her cheek. "Damn, you're soft. I have trouble keeping my hands off you."

Okay, serious melty stuff.

"What did you like about our scene?" he asked.

She flushed.

His hand that had been so gentle closed on her jaw and kept her from looking away.

"Uh. Everything?"

He snorted. "That's useful. You like breast clamps. Could I have made them tighter?" As if to illustrate, he moved his hand under the blanket and fondled her breast. When he pinched the nipple, she stiffened at the rush of pain—and pleasure.

"Answer me."

"I thought they were too tight at first, but then they were okay." She stopped and sighed when he raised his eyebrow for her to continue. "I liked the paddle, and I guess you could have hit harder, only I…"

He simply gazed at her, not laughing, not unhappy, just listening intently…and watching her. She looked down at her hands and admitted, "I've never come so hard before or felt so…" *Fulfilled.* "It was wonderful." When one of her buddies got her off during a scene, it felt like a pleasant burp. Satisfying enough, but she'd still have a hollow feeling—like receiving presents yet being alone at Christmas.

Firm fingers lifted her chin back up. "Simon knows you, so I figure you've played in Dark Haven before. What was the difference from other scenes?"

"How come I haven't seen you before?"

"I don't live here." He repeated, "What was the difference?"

He deserved the truth. "You pushed me." She stopped.

One cocked eyebrow was the response she got. *More.*

She exhaled and admitted, "You made me take it. I didn't get a choice, and I don't... It's different if I don't have any control." And he'd calmed her fears somehow. His overwhelming self-confidence and authority and that easy humor had gotten to her. God, she liked him.

Then again, experience said she'd proven lousy at differentiating a good man from a bad man. Really, she needed to go home now. A shrill scream from a nearby scene sent a chill through her, topping off her resolution.

She tried to slide off his lap, but his hand curved over her hip securing her in place. "Stay put, little sub," he growled. "What I'm hearing is that you like being pushed...if you feel safe. You like pain to some extent—having your ass paddled and nipple clamps on, and you liked getting off."

It sounded terrible when said out loud. "I don't want to talk about it."

He kissed her nose. "Considering I've had my hands all over you and my fingers inside you, how can talking embarrass you?"

She felt her face flame.

"A modest sub who likes to play in public. Interesting." He didn't grin often...but when he did, it was devastating. "You have any questions in turn?"

Her body had focused on the way he'd said, "*my fingers inside you,*" and the memory of how that felt; her brain couldn't concentrate on anything else.

"All right, I'll answer anyway. I didn't think I would, but I enjoyed beating on your ass. I enjoyed playing with you and getting you off. And I'd like to do more." His finger rubbed over her lips, parted them, and slipped inside.

Thick. Calloused. She swirled her tongue around it and sucked, delighted at how his eyes heated.

"I don't want to make love to you in front of all these people, Summer. Come back to my hotel, and we'll play there."

The unexpected request—and surge of fear—tightened her muscles, and she pushed his hand away. "No. I never play any-where but here. Ever."

"Ever," he repeated. "Does this have something to do with the bad experience Simon mentioned?"

She stiffened. "I won't talk about it."

"Uh-huh, that would be a yes." He shifted her closer, making it impossible for her to sit upright. "You're almost as easy to read as my little cousin."

"I need to go now."

"Woman, you're going to give me a complex if you keep trying to run away." His voice turned hard. "*Sit. Still.*"

Oh God. Why did he have to have such a willpower-destroying, subterranean baritone?

"You had fun—wonderful fun. And you like me." He paused and waited for her nod. "So although you don't want to go any-where with me, you'd probably like to continue?"

Chapter Four

VIRGIL WAITED, STRIVING for patience. Around them, the
dungeon pulsed with activity. The atmosphere had grown
darker, more serious. Much of the fancy submissive clothing had
disappeared; many of the subs were naked.

Seconds ticked away before the little sub nodded again. Satisfaction rolled through Virgil. In his younger days, he'd enjoyed so
many women that his father had been disgusted, but he'd learned a
few lessons. He damned well knew when a woman felt something
for him, and Summer did. They'd had a connection before he'd
spanked her, and it had grown stronger. He hadn't realized that
would happen. Pain and sex—he had a lot to learn if he continued.

But she trusted him, at least to a degree, this wary little sub who
reminded him of a skittish filly, and he had a feeling she didn't trust
many men, except maybe the ineffectual dom she'd hung out with
earlier. What had happened to her in the past? "If I asked you out
to dinner, would you go with me?"

"No."

Now that just hurt. "Do you date at all?"

"Not doms."

Obviously some bastard dom had been to blame. *No dating?* He
traced the tiny freckles on her cheeks with a finger. Well, he wasn't
looking to start a relationship anyway, especially with someone who
lived hours from Bear Flat. He'd come here only for this one night.

Tomorrow he'd head home, finish working out the plans for a greenhouse off the barn, and be back at work on Monday. He'd probably never see this little, sweet woman again.

The thought sent a pang of regret through him and increased his resolve to spend time with her now. "All right, then. I want more, and so do you, but you don't want to leave here. Am I hitting all the bases?"

"Yes." She had a seductively melodic voice, not low or husky, but…a little furry, as if she were purring. She could probably read a phone book and get a guy off.

"Then we'll stay put and play some more. Can we find somewhere here a tad more private?"

She bit her lip, which he'd noticed meant she was nervous. And between his kisses and her nervousness, her mouth was swollen. Tempting. He pulled her up and kissed her gently, then took his turn at nibbling on her lower lip. Soft. Velvety. Warm. Seductive as hell. Unable to resist, he took her mouth hard, plunging in and possessing. His cock thickened with his need to plunge into her pussy the same way.

What else would she let him do? What did he want to do?

Fuck, he wanted to do everything…

Her arms were around his neck when he pulled back, and her eyes were hot, dazed with desire. Why did she have to feel so right? "Find us somewhere to play, Summer. Now."

She blinked. "Maybe one of the theme rooms? They have windows, but we wouldn't be on display like this."

"That'll do."

He set her on her feet, and she hesitated. "You won't gag me, right?"

What the hell had that bastard dom done? "No, baby, I won't." He held his hand out, pleased when she set her hand in his. She didn't have an artist's long, slender fingers. Her fingers were short, her hand designed for work. He approved.

On the far end of the dungeon, Summer stopped in front of a

door and checked the window. "It's empty."

An actual room with a door. Amazing. "Seems private enough."

"Weeell." She flushed and pointed to small holes in the wall. "It's the Victorian theme room, so it has peepholes for voyeurs."

Jesus. "Let's take a look." He opened the door and guided her in. Eighteen-hundreds' brothel style. The flowery wallpaper in dark reds blended with deeply colored Oriental carpets. The four-poster bed held definite possibilities, especially with chains hooked up in the canopy frame. The wall sconces put out a soft yellow light. The bed curtains looked promising at first, but they'd been anchored to the posts so a person couldn't pull them around the mattress. Not that much privacy.

He glanced at Summer and paused. She obviously saw it different. Her color had faded, and her hands had a death grip on the blanket she wore.

"Is this too private for you, Summer?"

She inhaled slowly, looking more brave than excited. "I'm all right."

He hesitated. Should he continue in here? Perhaps so. She trusted him more than she had earlier…because he'd pushed her limits a little. Something else to remember. Being in here would push her too—as long as her fear didn't increase.

After setting the toy bag on the edge of the mattress, he smiled at her. "Hop up on the bed, sweetie. I have things I want to do to you."

Even in the dim room, he could see her eyes dilate, turning the sky blue to indigo. Anticipation…and submission. The knowledge squeezed his balls and sent a jolt of adrenaline through him.

Dropping her blanket, she climbed onto the high bed. Her hair glinted like starlight against the dark blue quilt, and he wanted to gather the silky strands in his hands. Soon. "Lie on your back."

She turned, propping herself up on her elbows, and his heart simply stuttered. Had he ever seen anyone more lovely? Her hair fell over her softly curved shoulders and upper arms. Beautifully creamy skin with a spattering of freckles across her upper breasts. Her stomach was rounded. His fingers remembered how her hips had felt in his grip.

He took his time. He'd never watched a woman in this way before, with the certainty she was his to look at as long as he wanted. Something inside him shifted with the knowledge.

Her lips were swollen. Her pale pink nipples were rosy from the clamps—her pussy bare. He wanted to taste her, there, where his fingers had stroked. And he didn't plan to wait any longer.

Her eyes met his, and she flushed prettily. He realized that if his inspection had embarrassed her, he didn't mind at all. In fact, he rather enjoyed it. But when he grasped her ankle, she shivered. *Slow down, Masterson.* She was excited but also frightened. How could he control her in the way she needed without terrifying her? He studied her and arrived at a compromise. "I'm not going to tie your hands. That should help with your worries."

She relaxed slightly, yet a little kissable pout indicated disappointment. *Perfect.* This might work. He walked around to the side of the bed. "Your hands will stay free, but I'm going to restrain your legs."

"What?"

How could a tiny tremor in her voice turn him on like someone had dumped a bucket of testosterone over him, yet seeing her truly scared had the opposite effect? And how the hell did he know the difference? But somehow he'd found her wavelength; he seemed to read her thoughts, her body. She was showing anxiety now, not fear.

And he liked her a little nervous.

Had he just thought that? He closed his eyes. *Fucking pervert.* What was he doing here?

Doing what I've wanted to do all my life. Looked like he was going to have a hell of a lot of thinking to do once he left Dark Haven. For now, though...

"Virgil?"

He squeezed her ankle and said smoothly, "Oh, you heard me." He unhooked a chain from the overhead canopy frame, raised her left leg, and clipped her ankle cuff to the dangling chain so her leg pointed straight up. She fought him, just the smallest amount, and the feeling of using his strength against her, overcoming her resistance, was heady stuff.

He knew if he didn't see that a little force excited her, he'd not enjoy it at all. But her nipples bunched even tighter. She wet her lips, her breathing fast.

He restrained her right leg so her legs were widely spread in a V shape. Her pussy was exposed—and facing the peepholes, which he didn't particularly like. That soft pink cunt was his and not for display.

"You're a beautiful woman, Summer." She blinked as if startled, then smiled.

He curved her hands around her inner thighs so it appeared as if she held herself open for him. "Keep your hands there and don't let go. No matter what."

Her breathing gave a nice hitch. Her nipples were hard peaks, and he pinched one lightly, making her hips wiggle. Fuck, he loved squirmy women. "Did you understand my instructions?"

She sounded as if she'd just finished a marathon as she said, "Yes, Sir."

The term pleased him more and more. Not only respectful, it was an acknowledgement of the connection between them. With a hand under her lush bottom, he lifted her and pushed a pillow under her hips to raise her pussy—and that little asshole—in the air.

How would she react when he tested that limit? His cock had its own reaction, trying to punch a hole through the front of his jeans.

From a small table, he took a packet of lube and a condom. He scowled at the rough calluses on his fingers, and then grabbed a glove too.

After kneeling on the foot of the bed, he let himself down onto an elbow where he could look at her pussy to his heart's content. The soft light showed her puffy outer lips glistening with her juices. Her legs were wide enough to open her inner folds, exposing her entrance as well. When he touched her, slickness coated his fingers, the finest compliment a man could get.

"You're all swollen and wet, sweetheart," he murmured. When he opened her labia farther, her thighs tensed.

With a finger, he stroked wetness from her entrance upward, making her legs jerk with each light brush over her clit. Her breathing changed, deepened, and he saw the muscles in her forearms tighten as she forced herself not to move.

Fuck, he could play with her all day, and he'd still want more. When she'd climaxed so hard before, it had been better than scoring a tie-breaking touchdown, than making a bull's-eye, than reaching a mountain peak. And he damned well wanted to make her come again. He bent his head and licked her, teasing with his pointed tongue. Under his mouth, her clit engorged, and the hood pulled back, leaving it totally vulnerable to his attentions.

She tasted like a day in July, hot and lightly musky, and when he grazed his lips over the crease between her hip and thigh, he breathed in vanilla and peaches. So very female, making him feel even more male. More dominant. Trapped in his jeans, his rigid cock strained to be free.

"Mmmm, you even taste like summer." He slid his tongue across her entrance and pushed his tongue into her. She half gasped, half moaned, and her legs jerked but were held fast. He'd dreamed of having a woman in this kind of helpless position where he could tease without her trying to distract him. He'd told himself he was a sicko.

But if he was, so was everyone else in this place.

She wanted what he had to offer; she trusted him with her body, her emotions. He'd give her everything he had...but damned if he'd hurry.

He set a hand just above her mound, pinning her down as he thrust his tongue into her cunt, then out to run over her clit. As her breathing turned erratic, the fragrance of her excitement increased. So did that…connection between them. It was like riding a wild mustang, forcing it to go where he wanted; reading its ears, its breathing, its muscles, and shifting his weight in response…enjoying the heady victory when it conceded he was the master. Right now, he could almost feel the sensations she was experiencing—and how her arousal was spiraling out of her control.

SUMMER FELT AS if she'd fallen into an inferno of need. Her fingernails bit into her thighs as she tried to keep from grabbing his hair and yanking him closer. "Please, please don't stop."

"You, little sub, don't have permission to speak, except for your safe word." He idly licked over her clit, then added, "I'm not a cruel man, so you can scream or moan if you must." He thrust his tongue inside her again and wiggled it.

Her eyes rolled back, and she whispered, "Oh God."

He rose up enough to shake his head at her in disapproval, and then studied her for a minute. "Dammit," he said to himself and lightly slapped the top of her mound, just missing her clit.

The abrupt sting shot down into her core, swelling every nerve until her entire pussy throbbed. She barely managed to close her mouth so only an "uhhhh" escaped.

He made a thoughtful noise, and she felt his finger pressing against her opening where her vagina was spasming from the pain…and the pleasure.

"Hell of a response," he muttered. "You got wetter." She heard a packet rip, rustling noises. Then his tongue came down on her clit, just her clit, flickering and circling. Pressure clenched inside her, and her muscles tightened. Every stroke of his tongue, hot and wet and determined, brought her closer…

Something pressed against her anus. *No.* "No. You—"

Another slap to her mound, and the sharp pain almost sent her over. Her head spun. Her pussy seemed caught in a vise of throbbing sensation.

"This won't be my *large* cock, honey." His chuckle was low as he added, "Just my finger." He didn't wait for her answer, but ruthlessly pushed harder until his slick finger slid past the ring of muscle.

He felt huge. A tremor ran through her at the feeling of him inside her, pressing deeper into the forbidden place. "I—"

His head lifted.

She hastily clamped her mouth shut and saw his lips quirk before he resumed.

Nerves sparked to life around the intrusion, joining the ones in her pussy, until her entire core pulsed with sensation.

Slowly his finger moved in and out of her back hole—and his tongue thrust roughly into her pussy in an entirely different rhythm. She trembled, unable to process anything as each touch demanded her attention. His tongue moved upward and onto her clit, stroke after stroke, until she moaned.

He gently tugged at the sensitive nub with his teeth, and sensation blasted through her. She gasped.

A rumble of laughter, and then his finger in her ass drove in deeper, and her hips jerked up, trying for more, trying for less. She had no control anymore.

He kept thrusting, hard and fast, and then closed his mouth over her clit, sucking in the same rhythm.

Every nerve in her body fired at once, and the massive explosion of sensation ripped through her, hot pleasure searing its way upward. She screamed. "Aaaa, aaa, aaah."

When the waves slowed and she could breathe, he sucked her clit into his mouth again. Her back arched, her pussy clenched harder than a fist. Her anus constricted around his invasive finger.

He didn't stop, and she moaned and wiggled and then broke

into almost hysterical giggles. "Stop. Oh God, please stop."

Oh, oh, goddammit. She'd spoken. He lifted his head, amusement glinting in his eyes as he raised the hand he'd been leaning on.

He smacked her mound sharply, and this time he hit her swollen clit...and at the same moment, he pushed a second finger inside her asshole.

"Noooooooo." Everything spasmed into a paroxysm of pleasure, and she came again, brutally intense.

A minute later, when he slid his fingers from her, her body clenched again, and she moaned. As she stared at the canopy above, it seemed to shimmer with every violent heartbeat. Sweat dampened her neck and breasts, and she couldn't stop gasping.

Note to self—don't talk without permission.

After sitting back on his heels, he disposed of the glove, then opened his jeans and rolled on a condom. Oh Lord, his cock was built like him, solid and big. Nicely long, but thick, thick, thick. He lowered himself between her legs, his body covering hers, his heavy weight erotic. His crisp chest hair teased her still-sensitive nipples to peaks, and she rubbed her breasts against him, wanting more.

He smiled into her eyes. "Every time you squirm, all I want to do is take you hard." He put his weight on his elbow and set one big hand on her breast. His thumb teased over the nipple and sent streams of sensation to her pussy.

The head of his cock rubbed against her entrance.

What was he waiting for? She tilted her hips up, trying to urge him on. He didn't move.

She frowned and met his eyes to see heat mixing with determination and authority. He had control.

"When I want to." He ran his finger over her lips. "You don't get a vote, honey."

The knowledge that she didn't have to try to decide what to do to please him was heady. Freeing. His will surrounded her, his eyes watched her, removing any chance of hiding her response to his touch. "Yes, Sir." *Take what you will. Take me.*

He smiled approval and leaned down. His hand lightly curved over her throat, not cutting off her air, but it still sent hot shivers rippling through her. His fingers were strong, warm, and then he took her mouth roughly. His hand on her neck kept her from moving, holding her in a totally submissive space as he dominated the kiss.

He didn't move away until her entire body lay limp under him. He nodded, satisfaction a gold color in his eyes. "Good. Put your hands on my shoulders," he said, his voice lower and rougher, vibrating against her bones. "Don't move them from there, is that clear?"

Oh God, he made her so hot. So wet. "Yes, Sir." Calling him that sounded right. She curled her fingers over his shoulders, feeling how his skin stretched over iron-hard muscles. She ran her hand down his deltoid, over the hollow in his triceps, and around to the curve of his biceps. He could do anything he wanted to her, she realized; he was just that strong. She stiffened, her fingernails digging into him in momentary fear.

His eyes narrowed, and just looking into them—at his face with his determined jaw, the laugh lines beside his mouth—her worry seeped away.

His slow smile warmed her. "Better. Now I want you perfectly still." His eyes crinkled as he whispered, "I'm going to fill you full, and you're not going to move as I do."

Oh God.

Before she had a chance to react, he was pushing into her. The head of his cock breached her entrance, so wide he had to slide in and out in increments before her muscles stretched to accommodate him. "Fuck, you're tight, baby."

The effort of holding still sent tremors up and down her body as he surged in farther. Wonderful, painful, thrilling stretching, more and more until his pelvis finally pressed firmly against hers. Every nerve throbbed, waiting for the delicious friction—

He pulled back, then thrust again, and she groaned at the exhilarating surge of sensation. Her fingers tightened on his shoulders, and he looked at her, eyes glowing with heat—and warning. "Don't move, Summer."

The need to control herself made everything so much more intense. Holding her breath, keeping so very still...

"That's a girl." His grin flashed.

Supporting himself on one arm, he used the other to lift her ass so he could rub his groin on her pussy with every stroke. The pressure, the brush of his hair over her sensitive clit, and the glide of his erection between her folds drove her mad, pushing her higher and higher until she couldn't help it and tried to grind against him.

"Summer," he warned.

"Oh please," she whispered, the size of him stretching her with each thrust. Her clit tightened, hardened, needing more, until her moans were almost constant.

When her head rolled on the pillow, he moved the hand bearing his weight up higher to tangle his fingers in her hair, trapping her. His weight pinned her body, she couldn't move her head, could only stare at his rugged face, feel his hand under her ass moving her to his own satisfaction.

As if he'd taken away her last barrier, a violent tremor ran through her. And then everything inside her clenched and burst outward. Hot pleasure engulfed her as her core spasmed around his intrusion.

He started a hard, fast rhythm, and the hammering of his shaft kept her orgasm going, drawing out the pleasure until the room lost focus. His hand pulled her hair painfully as he pressed deep, deeper. Under her fingers, his shoulders hardened, and he made a guttural sound. His cock jerked inside her as he came.

After a moment, he rested his forehead against hers, the movement so friendly and intimate that she sighed with happiness. He loosened his hand in her hair and nuzzled the damp strands at her temple. "Thank you, sweetheart," he said, his voice deep with satisfaction. "You'd be a delight in bed in normal circumstances, but when you"—he hesitated, as if uncomfortable with the word—"*submit*, the pleasure almost takes my head off. You're beautiful, Summer."

"Thank you, Sir," she whispered. As if he knew how comforting his closeness was, he stayed inside her a satisfyingly long time. Stroking his hand over her breasts and stomach, he kissed her now and then, letting her come back to reality surrounded by his warmth.

When she took a long shuddering breath, he gave her his slow smile and moved off, pulling his cock out with a sigh. After disposing of the condom, he released her legs, helping her work the kinks out. Then he lay down and pulled her against his side.

He smelled of sex and man and a hint of outdoorsy aftershave, and she sighed and settled her head in the hollow of his shoulder. She ruffled her fingers through his chest hair, tracing out the indentations of his nipples hidden within, and tried to think when she'd felt so satisfied. So content, as if every empty space in her body and soul had been filled to overflowing.

Eventually he kissed her forehead. "You sure you don't want to go back to my hotel room for a couple of hours?"

God. His unexpected question hit her hard, like he'd taken her lungs and squeezed the air out of them. She pushed up on her elbow. When he lifted her hand to his lips, she saw the tiny scars on her forearm where Dirk's cane had split her skin. Other scars decorated her back. Nothing too noticeable—perhaps she should be grateful for having pale skin—but always there. "No. I'm sorry, but no."

"All right." He opened her hand and laid it against his cheek. His light brown stubble scraped her palm, and his cheekbone was hard under her fingertip. Heavy bones, like the man, solid and unmovable. "Then will you meet me for breakfast? You can pick the place. I've got to return home tomorrow, but I want to see you before I leave." His brow creased. "There's... something...

between us. I'd like to come back and visit you."

She shook her head.

He gently tucked a lock of hair behind her ear, but his eyes had changed, golden brown to green, and already she knew the signs of his disappointment. Anger too? She tensed and examined his face carefully. He was a dom, used to getting his own way. Her gaze dropped to his hand as an echo of Dirk sounded in her head: "*Fucking bitch, you'll do it my way or else.*"

"I realize you don't know me well," Virgil said in an even voice, "but it bothers me when you look at me as if you believe I might hit you."

Her eyes flashed up to his, and she realized she'd been staring at his hand. Waiting for his anger. "I-I'm sorry, Sir."

"I think I get it. Did he beat you up more than once?"

"No," she said without thinking. "I mean—"

"Do not lie to me, Summer." Under her palm, the muscles of his face turned to steel. "That does piss me off, and considering your lack of clothing and your position, it would be easy to spank your ass again."

She stiffened, despite the wave of heat.

"Now, just so you know, I punched a girl once." His eyes narrowed in thought. "We had an all-out brawl, in fact."

The heat turned cold, and she started to pull away, but he laid his hand over hers, keeping it on his face. "She wanted only her friends on the merry-go-round, and I didn't think that was right. My brothers and I wanted to play too. She pushed me down and—"

Wait a minute. Merry-go-round? "Exactly how old were you?"

"About four." The sun lines at the corners of his eyes deepened. "Morgan told on me—the rat—and my father had a *discussion* with me about the Masterson philosophy of how a man treats a lady. It didn't matter how short the man was. Only a few things got Pa riled enough to wallop us, and I'd run square into that one."

"You were four." She stared at him, and laughter bubbled up, catching her by surprise. "You're such a jerk."

"Very true. But, Summer, that was the last time I hit a woman." His mouth turned up into a wry smile. "At least until recently."

Her muscles tightened again, and then she realized what he meant. "For BDSM."

He nodded. "My cousin fell in love with a dom, so I checked into it to see if I needed to kill him before they got married."

"And you liked it."

He sighed. "Yeah. Can't say I'm comfortable about the notion."

He massaged her fingers, his thumb rubbing over her knuckles. His hand felt so warm, she knew hers must be icy cold. She felt cold, in fact. *I'm not ready to be with a real dom.* He might be new, but he was damned well dominant.

"Does anything I've said change your mind about seeing me, Summer?" he asked softly.

She shook her head, the fear deeper than the unhappiness sweeping through her. *I want to...* "I c-can't. I'm sorry."

"And I'm sorry that I can't convince you to trust me, at least that far."

A discreet tap on the door made him look up, and he frowned. "We've hogged this room long enough, apparently." He rolled off the bed, picked her up around the waist, and set her on her feet. His strength still stole her breath.

He dressed faster than she did, nudged her hands away, and finished lacing up her vest. The feel of his sure fingers made her nipples harden, and he ran his finger over one, then kissed the top of her head. "Pretty Summer."

She didn't have any words to give him back.

After slinging his toy bag over his shoulder, he led the way out of the room. In the dungeon, he stopped. "Thank you for the evening," he said, his eyes shadowed by his hat. Looming over her, he tilted her chin up and gave her a kiss. A gentle, lingering, good-bye kiss.

She watched him walk away, saw how people automatically moved out of his path. So very dominant...and she wanted him back so badly her chest ached.

Chapter Five

V IRGIL'S DRIVE HOME to Bear Flat seemed to last forever. In the quiet of his truck, he couldn't evade the memories of the previous night and the beauty of Summer's responses. He had to face his own reactions and the unsettling realization that he'd known what to do to push her and how to take her further until she was aware of only him and the pain and pleasure he gave her.

With Summer, he'd learned what Logan meant by breaking down a submissive's barriers, opening her to the moment and to sheer pleasure.

He'd felt the joy in the exchange—they'd been so connected that he could almost hear her thoughts and feel the sensations she was experiencing. Knowing she'd willingly given him such power over her had been headier than drinking a bottle of scotch.

It felt good, but did that make it right? *Fucking-A.* He'd tied her up, taken her choices away from her, and dammit, that was wrong. His hands tightened on the steering wheel. He might be a tad overprotective when it came to women, but he damned well believed women were equal to men in everything except pure, dumb muscle. Hell, if he'd thought differently, his little cousin would have kicked his balls into his throat.

But he'd gloried in making Summer defenseless. In using his strength and size to do so. In seeing her try to escape his grip and his ropes.

She'd trusted him enough to let him tie her up even as she shivered, her eyes wide with a hint of fear and hot with lust. He'd watched her responses as he touched her, put cuffs on her, and his dick had been hard as a rock. He'd never been so aroused.

His mouth flattened. And then he'd spanked her...and liked it. Hell yes. It was as if an animal had been unleashed inside him. He'd heard the smack of the paddle hitting her ass, seen the shock of pain traveling through her, the tears puddling in her eyes. And he'd continued. What kind of a monster *was* he?

He'd told her he didn't hit women, even as her ass still glowed red from his actions. What a fucking hypocrite.

But she'd loved it. *"I've never come so hard before or felt so...fulfilled."* He'd given her what she wanted. More—she *needed* that pain, for whatever reason, and he'd fulfilled her need.

Hurting a woman isn't right.

But she'd wanted him to.

Hadn't she? Wasn't that what all rapists said? *She wanted it, your Honor, really she did.*

He turned onto the smaller county road leading to Bear Flat. The engine's hum deepened as the road grew steeper. The scent of pine filled the truck, and the air chilled with the bite of snow from the high peaks.

Home. He belonged here where the Mastersons had settled during the gold rush days and never left. His family had a reputation of honesty and uprightness. So did he. He took pride in being a cop—a good cop. So what kind of lawman got a rush out of tying up a woman and forcing her into *anything*—even pleasure? His gut tightened as if he'd eaten the lead pellets from a shotgun.

A few minutes later, he drove through his tiny town, nodding at the waves he received from people on the boardwalk. His neighbors. His friends.

Perhaps the Hunts could indulge in BDSM and still live here, but he didn't think he could, so it was best that Summer had turned him down. He'd had his fun, but he was home now. Time to set it aside and pick up a normal life.

ON SUNDAY EVENING, Summer finished a long bath and hesitated, then pulled on her pink flannel pajamas. Comfy wear for a body tender and aching from the previous night.

What a shame she had no comfy wear for her emotions. She'd spent the entire day thinking, getting more and more unhappy with herself. *Damn you, Virgil Whatever-your-name-is.* God, she didn't even know his last name. And she'd never see him again.

But because of him, she'd taken a good hard look at herself. Talk about depressing. Needing something to do with her hands, she dropped onto the couch and picked up her quilting hoop. She'd always thought of life as a winding stream…and hers had somehow diverted off into a bog. Gone stagnant.

Like in relationships. Here was Virgil, able to give her everything she'd ever dreamed of…and more. The excitement, the domination, the lust. She'd screamed. God—she'd actually screamed. Nothing had ever come close to what she'd experienced with him.

Could it be because she only played with her buddies—her risk-free dom friends. *You think?*

How long would she cling to the safe instead of going after what she really wanted? Scowling, she rocked the needle through the fabric. She'd turned into a sissy. *This isn't who I am. I'm the one who left everything behind in Nebraska to go to San Francisco.* The one who went to a BDSM club to explore needs which didn't run along a "normal" path.

But it had only taken one lousy—horrible—incident with an abuser to make her hide under the bed like a five-year-old hearing monsters in the closet. She'd sure ruined her chances with Virgil.

She turned the quilt frame and adjusted the material on her lap. Pretty pastels for her niece-to-be. She'd always wanted to have children. *Can't have children if you're afraid to make love with a man outside of a club.*

She snorted. Almost a year had passed since the incident. *You over the problem yet, Summer? Not.* She wasn't finding a cure on her own. After hauling in a long, deep breath, she made her decision. Tomorrow, she'd talk with Simon's submissive, Rona, who worked in hospital administration, and ask for help getting counseling.

That would fix her love life…maybe…but what about everything else? Aside from her friends, she wasn't happy with anything about her life.

Leaning back, she looked around at her apartment. At one time, she'd loved San Francisco, wondering at the variety of people and diverse little neighborhoods, the amazing ocean and pretty bay. But the excitement had slowly disappeared. Her apartment walls crept inward, crowding her. Despite the sunny color scheme, the wealth of potted plants, and the bright quilts tossed over the chairs, the rooms seemed dreary.

The apartment hadn't changed, though. She had. She glanced out the window, where the dull orange ball of the sun slowly sank behind…another building. Typical city sunset. In Nebraska, you could see just about forever, horizon to horizon—her lips twisted in a wry grin—and all planted in corn.

Go home? Her brother could always use more help on the farm, and the big, old farmhouse had room for their mother, him and his family, and Summer too, if she wanted. The nearby towns had hospitals with jobs for an experienced nurse.

I don't want to live in Nebraska; I like California. She just needed more space.

She nodded. Yeah. Farm girl needs a small town, one where she might afford a house. Have neighbors. Have a big garden. Have a dog… Just the thought made her yearn.

But this time, she'd be smarter about moving. First find a job, *then* she'd move. Not like before, coming here to live with her lover and getting dumped. She scowled at the ugly memory. The weight of her suitcase had matched that of her despair and fear: no money, no place to live, no job.

She'd never be so idiotic again.

So. First counseling. Then, once cured of the past, on to job hunting and a whole new life.

JANUARY IN THE Sierras. Not for the weak. Unlike the wet chill of a San Francisco winter, the mountains around Yosemite held a rip-the-air-out-of-your-lungs cold. But the wood stove in the tiny cabin at Serenity Lodge gave off plenty of heat.

Summer's fingers didn't tremble because of the cold.

She shook her head. *I've fallen off the edge into total insanity.* Wasn't her life chaotic enough? Over the past six weeks, she'd gone through counseling and job hunting. Then two days into her week of vacation, she'd interviewed and accepted a job in a Gold Beach hospital. Now she had to drive back to San Francisco, turn in her notice, get an Oregon RN license, pack, and move.

Detouring all the way to Yosemite to spend a weekend in the mountains was just plain stupid.

It was Simon's fault. He'd come to see her before she left for Gold Beach. *"Dark Haven is having a BDSM weekend at a mountain lodge. Since the owners are turning it into a family place, this is the last time the club will party there."*

She'd said no—like she had time to play? But then he dropped the bombshell: "Did you know that Virgil Masterson lives near Serenity Lodge?"

Virgil. She must have turned all sorts of colors, since Simon had busted out laughing. Then he'd said he'd reserve her a cabin—his treat—and would watch out for her. *"Rona and I both hope you'll come."*

Virgil. How could she not agree? She hadn't managed to get him out of her head. Not during the day, when every big man reminded her of him, and not during the nights, when she'd dream of how he'd tangled his hand in her hair, pulling her head back so he could take her lips. She'd hear his gravelly voice telling what to do. Quizzing her on how she felt. Rumbling a laugh. Every day, the need to see him hummed in her bones.

During the drive from Gold Beach, her anticipation kept increasing, totally overwhelming the excitement of the job offer.

Unfortunately they said he probably wouldn't attend the party—she needed to call and tell him she was here. And now the time had come, and she felt as if she had butterflies on steroids fluttering inside her chest.

She paced across the cabin. Paced back. Plopped down on the bed and stroked a hand over the handmade quilt. A traditional log cabin pattern. *Nice.* Maybe she'd sell them some of hers.

Stop stalling. She picked up the phone. Biting her lip, she dialed the number Simon had obtained from the lodge owner.

Ringing. Her hand tightened on the receiver. What if Virgil wasn't even in town? *Courage, girl.*

"Hello?" The man's deep voice was almost right but not rough enough, as if the jagged patches had been sanded out.

"Um. Virgil?"

"No, this is Wyatt. Hold on a sec." Thumping sounds, like boots, then, "It's for you."

Oh God, oh God. Summer rose to her feet. What if he—

"This is Virgil."

Her knees went weak, and she thumped back onto the bed. Her mouth opened. All the way here, she'd planned her speech. Not one of the smooth phrases came to mind. The butterflies must have eaten them.

"Hello?" His voice flowed over her in a flood of warmth.

"Um. Virgil." She swallowed. *You're a woman, not a little girl. Act like it.* "This is Summer. We met at—"

"Dark Haven."

Silence. As if he hadn't expected to hear from her again. Hadn't *wanted* to hear from her.

Oh God, this had been such a bad idea. "I'm sorry. I shouldn't have bothered you." She set the phone down. Carefully. The flutters in her chest stopped, falling into silence. Dead and gone.

"SUMMER?" VIRGIL SAID. *Silence.* Hell, she'd hung up. Cursing himself, Virgil thumbed the off button and checked caller ID. *Serenity Lodge.* Summer was here in Bear Flat?

At the sound of her voice—just her fucking voice—everything in him had surged forward like he'd dropped into first gear and stomped the gas. He throttled the feeling back. Hadn't he decided he'd avoid that lifestyle completely? Mastersons weren't perverts, dammit.

She's here in Bear Flat.

"Who called?" Wyatt still stood in the door of the kitchen. "Gorgeous voice."

"Nobody, so butt out."

"Yeah? You look kinda like *nobody* kicked you in the nuts," Wyatt commented. "Is she the brunette you dated last week, or the blonde the week before?"

Fucking small-town gossip. "No." *She's the one whose soft ass I reddened with a paddle. Warm Summer, full of laughter and courage, who's made every woman before and since seem dull and colorless. Damn him for ever walking into Dark Haven.*

"Then go get her, dumb-ass. Maybe if you get your rocks off, you'll stop being such an asshole," Wyatt snapped before stomping into his office.

Maybe so. His mouth dry as an August wind, Virgil got a glass of water and sipped it, staring out the window over the sink. From their mountain valley, the tall evergreens rolled upward…toward Serenity Lodge. What was she doing there, and how'd she get his number? Why now, after all this time?

His gut tightened. Was she in trouble?

He needed to talk with her. The thought felt right, a movement forward after weeks of spinning his wheels.

Gently, he set his glass down beside the tiny parsley plant Kallie'd left behind. The house had grown too damn quiet since she'd married Jake. She seemed happier than he'd ever seen her, and he bet he'd get a niece or nephew soon, but he missed her.

The plant's curly leaves drooped, looking a hell of a lot like he'd felt for weeks now, ever since Summer kicked him to the curb. He carefully poured water into the pot. *Live, little guy.*

He knew he'd been acting like the asshole Wyatt called him. And not because of any ego bruising. The problem was she'd been more than just a quick fuck to him.

They'd connected. Everything she'd done had reverberated through him, had felt *right*—like on the target range when form and breathing and vision all came together, and even before he'd pull the trigger, he'd know it was a bull's-eye. Being with her felt *right*.

The need to see her gnawed at his gut.

He must have hurt her feelings with his flat-footed response to her voice. Not good. He'd best explain, face-to-face, why he couldn't pursue a kink like BDSM.

What if she'd actually come to see *him*? Wanted to be with him?

His cock stood right up and begged.

Fucking-A. He could almost feel her small hands gripping his biceps as he thrust into her, hear her hoarse voice begging him, "*Oh please,*" see her eyes, wide and anxious and wanting to please him. Nothing else and no one else had ever come close to making him feel like that.

But I'm not a fucking pervert, dammit. Hadn't he already figured all this out?

Nonetheless. He'd go to her. He'd explain. Maybe they could still see each other. Without the kink.

Without stopping to change out of his uniform, Virgil jumped in his truck and headed up the mountain. Night had fallen; the air had chilled with the sharp scent of snow riding on the wind. As the headlights illumined the road before him, and each mile brought back more memories of Summer, his resolutions started to snap like dry branches in a winter storm.

Chapter Six

W HEN SUMMER OPENED the cabin door, all Virgil could do was stare. Weren't dreams supposed to be better than reality? But the sight of her hit him like a heart-stopping kick to the chest.

She was so beautiful, with the sun-colored hair he wanted to gather into his hands, the little freckles over her creamy skin, the wide blue eyes that matched the color of her fluffy sweater.

"Virgil. What are you doing here?" Her expression blanked, but he'd seen the flash of stunned delight in her eyes.

He stepped forward, forcing her to retreat, and closed the door behind him. Jesus, Mary, and Joseph, just seeing her loosened his grip on reality. "I want to talk to you."

"No need. I shouldn't have bothered you—it was a momentary mind-blip." Her voice shivered along his nerves, and he hardened.

"A blip, huh?" Oh, he could tell it was more than that. Her eyes were vulnerable. Needy. She wanted him as fucking much as he did her.

The room held only one chair. He pulled her over to the twin beds, motioned for her to sit on one, and he took the other, trying to forget how she'd squirmed under him last time they'd enjoyed a mattress. "We're going to talk anyway."

"You're married or involved or something, right?"

He stared at her, then snorted. "Now that's just insulting,

woman. No, none of those."

"Oh. Well."

How the hell to explain, especially when he kept wanting to cuff her hands behind her back, set her on her knees, and watch the yielding look come into her eyes. "I did a lot of thinking after leaving Dark Haven and again tonight, so let me lay it out for you." He cleared his throat. "Tying up women, beating on them... It just doesn't seem honorable. Coming back from San Francisco, I decided it wasn't a good...hobby...for me."

Her gaze dropped to where his shearling jacket hung open, revealing his uniform. His badge. His weapons belt. "That's not a costume, is it?"

"'Fraid not."

She bit her lip, and dammit, he wanted to be the one nibbling. "I can see that would be a problem," she said.

"After you called, I thought about it, figured maybe we could see each other like normal people. Vanilla, right?" He wanted her in a way he hadn't experienced ever. Was this craving what addicts felt—an ache deep inside?

"That's non-BDSM, yes."

"Trouble is"—the words spilled out, his brain definitely disengaged—"I remember too well how you look when you're restrained, how you pull against the cuffs, how you whimper..."

Pink flushed her cheeks, and the next breath she took was deeper. "Virgil—"

Dammit. Had he really thought he could just kick over the need for more. Did he really want to go through his life having "vanilla" sex, never getting the fullest sense of satisfaction?

No.

Pa had always said, *"If you can't change your mind, why have one?"* Logical enough, but not particularly comfortable when his mind did a complete one-eighty and left him in the dust. He ran his finger along her jaw, so soft and sweet, and gave her the uncomfortable truth. "I don't think I can be with you and not push for your submission. Might be different if you hated it, but you like—need—it. You liked when I held you in place, when I restrained your wrists. You wanted more."

"Yes." Her voice came out a whisper.

The room had turned hellishly hot. "You called me. You want to play."

She nodded.

He sat back. *Cool down, Masterson.* "Maybe we can compromise. Bear Flat is a small town. The Serenity Lodge parties are an open secret, but no one minds, since the Hunts keep their kinkiness to the Lodge and to outsiders who come here to play—and spend money." He took her hand, curling his fingers over hers, running his thumb over the tiny calluses on her palm. He wanted those hands on him. "But I'm not an outsider. And I'm supposed to enforce the law, not indulge in what people figure are orgies."

"Orgies and cops. Not a good combination." She tried to tug her hand away.

"Summer, I would very much like to play again. But not publicly." If he kept touching her, he'd be on top of her. He rose and paced across the room. "In all reality, honey, I don't like the exhibition stuff. What I do with and to you is private. I don't want to share any of it. I don't want others to see you naked, to see how you glow when you're aroused, to hear you when you come. That's mine."

SUMMER STARED AT him as his words shook something deep inside her. She started to nod, and then the meaning of what he said registered. She'd be alone with him—she *was* alone with him. Fear rose, crested, and broke over her. The cabin chilled as if a wind had blown out the fire in the stove. "No."

"No?"

"No. I can't." So big, he was too big. Dear God, no one knew he was here. She rose, trapped between the two beds.

"Summer, look at me."

Her back hit the wall of the cabin. She stared at his hands, his huge hands. He could beat her. He could—

"Eyes. On. Me." He snapped. "Now."

Her gaze shot to his.

"You're seeing the past, honey, not me," he said gently, not moving at all. "Have I ever hurt you"—his smile flickered—"in a way you didn't like?"

She swallowed, and her heart rate slowed. "No."

"Do you really think I would?"

"I—" Her hands clenched in front of her. "I didn't think he would either."

"Ah." Virgil sighed and leaned back against the door, obviously assuming a relaxed posture. "So he not only hurt you, but now you don't trust your own judgment either?"

"Just go. Please, Virgil. This will never work."

He hesitated like he'd argue, then nodded and left.

As he walked out, Summer choked on a sob. *No. Come back!* Fear drained out of her, leaving only emptiness behind. He'd wanted a compromise, to try, had talked honestly, and she'd panicked. Counseling hadn't done her any good at all. She'd been so hopeful. So sure she was cured.

She stared at the door, wishing with everything in her for him to walk back in…and knowing she couldn't function if he did.

Why am I even here?

The cabin resonated with loneliness, and her eyes filled. She'd failed. Why bother staying any longer? She had things to do, an apartment to pack, a move to make. Tears dripped on her clothing as she tossed the few items she'd unpacked into the suitcase. After her voice steadied, she'd call Rona so she and Simon wouldn't worry.

She stepped out the door. Snowflakes flitted through the air, invisible in the dark night, but glittering in the lantern lights marking the path. By morning, the mountains would be dusted with white. What would it be like to lie in bed with Virgil, watching the snow come down?

She'd never know. Hefting the suitcase, she trudged to her car. *Stupid. Such a coward. I should have tried harder. But a relationship never would have worked. But how would—*

"You always run when you're nervous?" Virgil's gentle deep voice stopped her. Her head jerked up.

He rested his hip against a big pickup in the parking area, arms folded over his chest.

Her heart did a painful somersault. "What are you doing here?"

His slow smile creased his face. "Considering all your muttering, probably the same as you. Wanting to stay, telling myself to leave."

"To stay? Why?"

"Well, I figured once I got home, I'd call and talk you into an early supper tomorrow. But I changed my mind." After tugging her case away, he set a hand in the small of her back and guided her toward her cabin. "We'll play here tonight in the lodge so you'll have people around you. Tomorrow we'll see where we're at."

"But...your reputation."

His mouth tightened. "Will have to take care of itself." He looked down at her, pulling her closer until her hips rubbed against his. "We've got more between us than a night of screwing around, so I guess I can handle being called a pervert, if need be. You know, even after this long, I still wake up thinking of you and go to sleep thinking of you."

Oh God. Her eyes prickled with tears. She'd considered herself silly, like a love-struck teenager, but he felt the same way. How many men would have admitted that?

But she needed to stop the hope rising in her. "Virgil, I had counseling after we—after I wanted to leave Dark Haven with you and couldn't. I thought I was cured, but I still panicked in the cabin. I don't see how this could work."

"Well now, appears I turned your life as upside down as you did mine," he said softly. His knuckles rubbed across her cheek in a gentle caress, his fingers warm against her cold skin. "Did your counselor say you were all fixed when you were done?"

"Uh." She blinked, remembering the last session. A glimmer of hope lightened her heart. "I forgot. She said the panic attacks might still happen, but they'd get better, especially if I keep working through them."

"Ah-huh. Would you like help working through them?" His eyes challenged her.

He'd risk his reputation for her? Could she give less? Her spine straightened. "Yes."

"There we go, then."

At the cabin, he opened the door. When she stepped in, he smiled and ran a finger over her lips. "I'll wait in the lodge. If you have one of those corset things, I'd like to see you wear it. No underwear, please."

After setting her suitcase on the floor, he closed the door behind him.

She stood, a little stunned. He was like a river current, cradling her gently until she tried to break free, only to realize it inexorably carried her downstream. Here she was, back at the cabin, ready to change into what he'd told her to wear.

Why did that feel so exactly right?

WHEN SUMMER ENTERED the lodge, the party was in full swing. She stopped to gawk. Sometime since she registered, the owners had transformed the rustic main room into a shadowy dungeon. Heavy iron chains dangled from bolts in the log walls and dark rafters. Bulbs flickered redly in the wall sconces. Two X-shaped St. Andrew's crosses held submissives. Another sub hung in suspension in the center of the room. Closer to the end wall, a dom was using his sub in a leather swing...quite vigorously. A flogger kept time to the music of Type O Negative's erotic "Love You to

Death."

Wow. Simon's party last year was the only private play she'd ever attended, and this was as different from his stately mansion as anyone could imagine.

Near the door, one of the lodge owners, Logan Hunt had his arm around a lushly curved redhead while he spoke with a man and woman in street clothing. Summer frowned. With dark brown hair, strong features, and intensely blue eyes, the two men must be brothers. But why did they seem familiar? Come to think of it, so did Logan's woman.

He motioned her over. "Summer, this is my wife, Rebecca."

The redhead smiled. "Nice to meet you. I like your corset.

Summer grinned. Aside from the color, there was no difference between her blue corset and Rebecca's green one. "Yours too."

Logan set his hand on his wife's stomach. "This is the last time she gets to wear it—she needs room for other things."

A baby? No wonder the owners planned to turn Serenity into a family lodge. As Rebecca flushed, Summer felt a squeeze of envy. "Congratulations."

"And this is my brother Jake, and his wife Kallie," Logan said.

The tiny brunette smiled, and Jake said, "It's good to see you looking so well, pet."

That voice, those blue eyes… "Have we met before?"

"Ha. Like I said—you're totally forgettable." Logan grinned at his brother.

Jake scowled back, then took her hand gently. "We met at Simon's party last year. I held you after your bastard date caned you."

She flinched and tried to pull her hand away.

His eyes narrowed. "Simon said you're doing better."

One slow breath and she'd regained her equilibrium. *Nice reaction, Ms. I've-been-cured.* Well, no wonder he seemed familiar. She remembered how he'd wrapped her in a blanket, cuddled her, and made her drink tea until she'd stopped shaking. "Sorry, you took me by surprise. That night isn't a fond memory."

"I'd say not," Rebecca spit out. "I wanted to hit the guy so bad, but these two wouldn't let me." She gave Logan a dirty look, then added, "But if no one told you, they each took a punch—that's after Simon broke his nose—then threw him out the front door so hard he bypassed the sidewalk and landed in the street."

What a lovely image. Summer realized she was smiling. "Thank you. Thank you all."

"Wish I'd been there," Kallie muttered. Her dark eyes snapped with anger. "I hate bullies."

"Easy there, sprite," Jake said. He grinned at Summer. "We won't be here this weekend, but I wanted to make sure Simon wasn't lying." He touched her cheek gently. "You look good. Some dom will be a lucky guy."

She flushed. "Thank you."

"Simon says Virgil's got his eye on her," Logan said casually.

Kallie's mouth dropped open. "Virgil? Really?"

"Good job, asshole," Jake said to Logan and slung his wife over his shoulder. "We're out of here, little snoopy person."

"Wait, dammit. I want to—" The door closed behind them, Kallie still protesting. A man's shout of anger came through the door.

Logan snorted. "I think she bit him." Rebecca buried her face in his shirt, giggling her head off.

"Ah…am I missing something?" Summer asked.

"Small town," Logan said. From the dom's uninviting expression, he wouldn't explain further. "Off with you. Virgil went upstairs to change clothes. I don't know if he's come down yet."

"Right."

Virgil wasn't in the dungeon area.

In the kitchen, MaryAnn stood by a munchie-loaded counter, nibbling and singing along with Peter Steele's dark voice: "Am I good enough…for you." She gave Summer a happy smile. "'Bout time you got here. I thought I'd have to freeze my ass off to go pry you out of your cabin."

"A friend stopped by."

"Really? Master or slave?" MaryAnn picked up a sugar cookie and took a bite.

Kallie isn't the only snoopy person. "A dom I met in Dark Haven last month."

MaryAnn's eyes widened. "You're seeing someone besides those buddies of yours? About time, girl."

Jeez. "What's wrong with my friends?"

"Nothin', but you got no buzz with them." MaryAnn toasted her with the bottle. "So who's this other dude? Are you dating him? Is he nice?"

"He's nice." *Wonderful, exciting, awesome.*

"Sounds like a *but* coming."

"But he doesn't want to scene in public. And I don't—I can't—I won't play in private." She picked up a bottle of water and unscrewed the top. "It's hopeless."

"Girlfriend, if you figure he's such a jerk in private, why would you play with him at all?"

"I don't think that. I just don't know." The swallow of water stuck halfway down, and Summer coughed. "It's like, even if a guy's all sweet in public, he could go off on you when you're alone together. How can you know?"

"Not easy. Course, I like'em nasty, and I've got one waiting in there now." MaryAnn headed out, squeezing past Simon and Rona, who stood in the doorway. From their concerned expressions, they'd heard Summer's worries.

"I spoke with Logan about your cop." Simon walked over to squeeze her shoulder reassuringly. "He was raised here, and he's well-respected. His cousin married Jake Hunt. According to Kallie, he's honest, caring, blunt, and overprotective."

Kallie was his cousin? No wonder she'd been curious. "Information helps. Thank you, Sir."

Rona put an arm around her waist. "It helps intellectually, but until you know he's safe at gut level, nothing will ease your fears, right?"

"No." Summer sighed. "But—"

"There you are." Virgil walked into the kitchen, dressed in jeans and a black T-shirt that appeared sprayed over his muscular chest. His biceps stretched the sleeves in such a way she wanted to take a little bite. Oh, she definitely wanted to play with him.

He nodded at Simon and Rona, then leaned a hip against a counter. His gaze traveled from her loose hair, her mouth, lingered on the cleavage created by the corset, dropped to her thighs displayed by her short latex hoop skirt, and down to her bare feet. His brow creased. "You didn't walk here barefoot, did you?"

Rona laughed and whispered in Summer's ear, "He's definitely a protective one," then dragged Simon out of the room.

"No, I have snow boots," Summer answered. God, just looking at him made her shake inside.

"You know, you haven't kissed me yet." He pulled her forward into his arms. Iron-hard arms, a rock wall of a chest. Why such an embrace seemed warm and soft and wonderful was one of life's great mysteries. She pressed her face into his neck, inhaling the lingering scent of the leather jacket he'd worn, his light, woodsy aftershave, and his own masculine fragrance.

With a rumble of pleasure, he pulled her between his legs. Her pelvis bumped his thick erection, and she rocked into it, mesmerized by the feel, wanting him inside her.

Chapter Seven

WHY DID SHE feel so fucking right? Virgil wondered. He threaded his hands through her sunshine-and-silk hair and kissed her lips lightly, breathing in peaches and vanilla and woman. His cock throbbed, demanding action. "We're going to go play, but first, let me run over your limits. No blood sports, no severe pain."

"No anal."

He shook his head and smiled when her eyes widened. "You liked my fingers in your ass, honey. Why do you think you wouldn't like my cock there?"

"I just know."

"No, you don't." From the way her body had reacted to that slight amount of anal play, he figured she'd love more. If not, he wouldn't either—perhaps she didn't understand that.

She bit her lip, but her eyes had turned the color of larkspur blooming in the mountain meadows. His mother had loved larkspur. And laughter and courage. She'd have approved of this tough, joyous woman.

He ran his hands over Summer's smooth, bare shoulders, down her tightly laced corset, and curved his fingers under her soft, soft ass cheeks. If he got any harder, he'd toss her onto the huge oak table in the center of the kitchen and take her right there. "You're going to try anal once, and if you don't like it, then you'll have a reason to say no."

The way her body melted under his touch said she'd accept his will; the heat in her eyes said she wanted to.

When she whispered, "Yes, Sir," pleasure and power flooded his veins. He had to face it—his need to dominate equaled her need to submit.

AN HOUR LATER, Summer considered kicking Virgil somewhere painful. *Frustrated much, Summer?* She'd expected him to drag her off and do a scene. Instead, they'd strolled around the room and watched the various sessions. After the third one, she caught the way he was studying her reactions.

At a heavy flogging scene, she'd tensed up, and he'd pulled her closer. "Not your thing, I know. Not mine, either."

When watching a threesome, he'd smiled at her and run a finger down her cheek. "Doesn't do anything for you, does it? Me either. I'm too possessive."

Near the center of the room, he deliberately stopped to watch a dom taking his sub from behind—in the ass.

The woman moaned and wiggled as her dom pushed deeper. Summer felt her nipples bunch into peaks, and her pussy grow damper. She glanced up.

Virgil's focused gaze rested on her, not the scene. "You're flushed, sweetheart," he murmured. "Are you thinking about being in that position tomorrow? Taking your master's cock in a very, very private place."

Her asshole tightened, making her quiver. And making her even wetter.

He smiled slowly. "Oh, you are. You'll take it, and I won't stop until you come."

God. Her skin seemed to shimmer with heat. She looked away and spotted MaryAnn.

The submissive swaggered up to Virgil. "Hey, Master, are you looking for a fun sub?" She ran a finger over his biceps and batted her thick, black lashes.

His brows drew together in displeasure. "Thank you, no." He turned back to Summer.

"But—" MaryAnn moved closer and rubbed her breasts against his arm.

Summer stared. MaryAnn never came on to the doms. What was she doing?

Virgil's voice was colder than the mountain air as he snapped, "Leave."

MaryAnn stepped back hastily. After shooting Summer a bemused look, she walked away.

Virgil shook his head. "I thought Dark Haven's submissives were better behaved." He put his arm around Summer. "Let's see if you have a liking for anything else."

"I already told you what I'm into."

"No, honey, you only gave me what you don't like." He took her mouth for a long, thorough kiss.

More, more, more. She set a hand on her stomach, trying to control her breathing. "Do I get to know your preferences?"

He chuckled. "I'm male. I like sex. I'm a dom—although it still feels wrong to say that—so I like control." He put his hands around her waist and lifted her to stand on a low coffee table. Her eyes were even with his.

"Virgil!"

"I like your taste...everywhere. I like the heat of your cunt around my cock or around my fingers." He slid his hand under her skirt and between her thighs, and when his finger pushed up into her, she moaned.

He gave a satisfied rumble. "I like the sounds you make." His teeth closed on her shoulder. The small bite of pain rippled through her, and her pussy clenched around his finger. She inhaled sharply.

"Yeah, that sound." His breath bathed her ear. "Whimpers. Moans. Screams. Little panting noises and sighs. You have the most beautiful voice I've ever heard."

The hot flush rolled up her neck to her face. She tried to edge away.

His hand fisted in her hair, tugging her head back so her eyes met his. He held her in place as he slid another finger inside her entrance, thrusting gently as his thumb pressed on her clit. *Oh God.*

"That sound right there," he said in the rough, devastating voice she still heard in her dreams. "Give me more."

His thumb circled her clit.

They stood right out in the middle of the room. A dom walking past paused to watch for a second. Summer shook her head. "Virgil, no."

His eyes drew her in, swept her willpower away. Without answering, he lifted his knee and used his boot to nudge her feet farther apart on the low coffee table, spreading her more open. "Personally, I like privacy," he said softly. "I prefer that I'm the only one to hear those little sounds you make—but if you like to share, then you will."

With his fingers in her, his hand in her hair, she couldn't move as he mercilessly aroused her. His thumb pressed harder, teasing the hood over her engorged clit. Her toes curled and her hands fisted as the pressure in her center tightened, as each slow thrust increased the sensations. He bent his fingers, moving to a new spot with each penetration until they rubbed against a...*place.*

One that sent her senses spiraling away. She could feel the climax advancing toward her. "Oh, please. God, please." She grabbed his upper arms, and his rock-hard biceps flexed under her grip.

"Let it happen," he murmured. His fingers pulled out and drove in forcefully. Once. Twice. His thumb brushed over the very top of her clit.

The dam broke, and scalding pleasure flooded her system in a massive rush of sensation. Her back arched as she went up on tiptoes. He released her hair, setting his hard hand against her bottom, holding her so the fingers of his other hand could continue.

Each slow, slick stroke made her clench inside, sending more surging pleasure through her.

As her knees started to give, she let out a long moan that lightened his eyes with satisfaction.

"Very pretty. I hadn't heard that one before." Taking pity on her, he lifted her off the table and wrapped his arms around her, holding her against his solid body, a mountain no force would move.

She rested her forehead on his chest. She had gotten off so thoroughly her fingertips still tingled...and she craved doing it again. "I want you inside me," she whispered. She wanted the intimacy—him giving and her giving and...

"I'm not one to fuck a woman in public, Summer." The coarse words hurt, but then he added, "And when it's more...more special...it's even more difficult."

"Oh." He'd given her a wonderful orgasm, held her so sweetly now. She'd never wanted to please a dom so much, and instead she kept letting him down. The guilt grated against her soul. "I'm sorry. I didn't—"

"Shhh." He nuzzled her cheek, his jaw scratchy with a man's heavy stubble. "It's not your fault. We'll figure something out, baby." He tucked her hair back, exposing her face. "You are so pretty when you're all pink."

As relief eased the remorse, she kissed him, willing him to understand how much it meant he didn't blame her. "Thank you."

He snorted. "I intend to take my annoyance out of your hide one way or another."

Somehow his threat didn't worry her at all. She snickered.

"Brat." When he let her go, her legs wobbled like an old woman's. With a huffed laugh, he sat her on a couch. "Stay here while I get you some water."

As Virgil disappeared into the kitchen, Simon appeared and pulled Summer to her feet. "Don't talk. Just come with me." He stopped right outside the kitchen and positioned Summer where she could see inside.

With his back to the door, Virgil faced MaryAnn in the otherwise empty kitchen.

"Oooh, it's the big dom," MaryAnn cooed.

"Find someone else, girl." The cold, rough voice should have sent any submissive fleeing.

Not MaryAnn. The brunette ran her fingers down Virgil's chest.

He gave a grunt of exasperation and brushed her hands away. "You trying to get in trouble?"

"I like trouble." MaryAnn actually moved closer and rubbed his crotch.

Summer scowled at the bite of jealousy. *That's mine.*

With an irritated snort, Virgil pulled handcuffs from his pocket, spun MaryAnn around, and cuffed her wrists behind her back. Oh yeah, the man was definitely a cop.

He fisted MaryAnn's braids tightly enough to make her squeak and frowned down at her.

Summer crammed her hand into her mouth. What if he hit her? She pushed at Simon. "Go help."

Simon shook his head and gripped the back of her neck. "Stay put, pet."

She hesitated.

Before Summer could decide what to do, Virgil pushed the handcuff key between MaryAnn's lips. "Ask Simon or Logan to free you and return my cuffs." As if the sub no longer existed in his universe, he pulled the refrigerator door open.

Simon chuckled. "Rona said you needed to see to believe. Now get back to the couch."

Summer stared at him. Had Simon told MaryAnn to deliberately provoke Virgil?

MaryAnn appeared in the door, snickering under her breath.

"You sneaks," Summer whispered, and the two conspirators

grinned.

Simon jerked his head, and Summer ran for the couch.

She dropped onto it, and a second later, Virgil reentered the room. His gaze found her with palpable warmth, before he walked over to where Simon was uncuffing MaryAnn.

As she waited, Summer curled into a corner of the couch to think. MaryAnn had made Virgil mad, and he'd merely sent her to Simon. He could easily have lost his temper and gotten very rough. Some doms would have.

"Earth to Summer." Virgil's amused voice came from a foot away.

"Oh!" Her head jerked up, and she put her hand over her heart to make sure it hadn't stopped. "Sorry."

He tore off the plastic seal and opened the water bottle with that ingrained courtesy of his. Well, when he wasn't holding her immobile and driving her into an uncontrollable orgasm. In the center of the room.

After handing her the water, he picked her up and sat down on the couch with her in his lap. She shifted to get settled, felt his thick, very hard cock, and squirmed more, until he growled and held her hips still.

"Oh sorry." She couldn't suppress her giggle.

"Evil girl." He drank some of her water and then leaned back with a sigh.

His arm around her was firm, holding her against his big chest, making her feel safe...and...and *wanted*. But she hadn't given him anything in return except doubts and fears. And he didn't know if he even liked being a dom. Another twinge of guilt assaulted her. "Does it bother you to...to make me do things?"

"Some." From the underlying grimness in his voice, he definitely felt uncomfortable. "How about you? Does it bother you when I force you into something?"

"Well, I didn't want to stand on a coffee table. But you made me, and that turned me on even more." She took a breath. How could she explain? "Sometimes there's an empty place inside me. Cold. When you take charge, it seems to fill that up. Warms me— even if what we're doing has nothing to do with sex."

His arms tightened, pulling her so close his heartbeat thudded through his ribs to hers. "Well. That's a bit of how I feel when I know I've satisfied you and know you're happy because of me."

Thank God. If he hadn't liked being in control, she couldn't have gone on. She had a thought. "You started because of your cousin, but before—did you ever think about bondage or domination?"

"Oh yeah." The corner of his mouth turned up. "When I tied you up during the calf roping, you definitely fulfilled a fantasy. And we knocked off a few more later."

That felt good. "Uh, would it help to know I've always wanted this?" She ran her hand over his strong jaw and saw, as usual, he was giving her all his attention.

"Always?"

"Pretty much. My Ken doll used to tie Barbie up and spank her for being bad."

He choked.

She grinned and whispered, "I had a Bondage Barbie."

When his growling laughter burst out, she snuggled closer in perfect contentment.

▲

"BONDAGE BARBIE." VIRGIL would never look at the damn doll the same way again.

He made Summer finish her water, although when she sat up, he'd swear she intentionally squirmed her ass on his cock.

If she kept teasing him, he'd fuck her here on the couch, privacy or not.

But during their tour of the room, he'd spotted a likely place. "Up you go." After rising, he curved his fingers over her nape, his hand big enough to get a good grip. Not a bad technique, although he'd noticed a collar like Rebecca wore gave even more control.

He guided his pretty little sub to the back corner. Two over-stuffed chairs faced a tall couch that screened the area. He stopped Summer in front of one chair. "Kneel here."

She gave him a startled look, and then gracefully sank to her knees. She assumed the eyes-down, knees-apart, hands-on-thighs position he'd seen other subs use.

She hadn't knelt like that in the club, he realized. A dark satisfaction filled him, the knowledge she wanted to please him even more now than then. "Sweet Summer," he murmured.

Although her gaze stayed on the floor, a happy smile flickered over her lips.

By unscrewing the light bulb in a wall sconce, he plunged the area into shadowy darkness. *Much better.* In the center of the room, Logan frowned and turned to look. When Virgil raised his hand, the lodge owner nodded acknowledgement.

Virgil returned to Summer and noted the difference the change of lighting had accomplished. She was quivering with excitement and nerves. He knew just how to up the tension some more. "Strip, please."

"Yes, Sir," she whispered. When she rose and started to un-hook her corset, his cock felt as if someone had closed a hot fist around it. He dropped into the chair and watched silently as her mouth-watering breasts came into view, then her softly rounded stomach. Fuck, she was beautiful.

All too soon, she set her clothing on a chair and stood before him, eyes cast down, shifting her weight from one foot to another. Adorably uncertain.

The small amount of light glinted off her blonde hair and brushed over her smooth skin. It shadowed beneath her full breasts and created a tempting darkness between her thighs. "Present yourself. Feet shoulder-width apart, hands behind your back."

Unfortunately, the dim lighting meant he couldn't see the flush rising into her face, although he could almost feel it. The position opened her legs nicely and raised her breasts—no wonder doms liked it so much. Her nipples had peaked into tiny spears. He pulled her forward until her toes touched his. "Bend and hold on to my shoulders."

Her small hands closed on his shoulders, sending a punch of lust straight to his crotch. As he'd figured, her position dangled her breasts in front of him like hanging fruit. He took one nipple in his mouth, teased the point to even greater hardness, and sucked strongly. Her breath caught.

When he gently closed his teeth on the tender tip, a shudder ran through her. Yes, she liked that. Not releasing her breast, he grasped her arms and kept her in place, then laved the peak and bit down again. Carefully. Firmly.

She moaned, her eyes half-closed, her skin hot under his hands.

He blew air over the wet nipple. "You have beautiful breasts, honey. I remember how they look when they're swollen and red." His voice came out rough with his need.

Her whisper was only hint of sound. "Yes, Sir."

"I'm not going to tie you down. I expect you to stand perfectly, completely still…no matter what I do." He released his grip on her arms and took her left nipple in his mouth. So velvety soft with tantalizing bumps surrounding the slightly rough tip. He teased and sucked, and it swelled under his attention. With his fingers, he played with her other breast, teeth on the left, lightly pinching the right.

Her grip tightened on his shoulders. When he bit down, he heard a whimper of mingled pain and need. Her whole body shook, but she didn't move, didn't try to pull away. "You're such a good little sub," he murmured. "Open your legs for me."

The helpless sound she made increased the hum in his veins and the pressure in his already rock-hard cock. As she moved her feet apart, he inhaled the scent of aroused female. He brushed his knuckles down her soft stomach to her mound, then ran one finger over her bare pussy. Very, very smooth. "Did you think of me when you shaved today?"

A hesitation. "Yes, Sir."

Why did her whispered answer remind him of the last shoplifter he'd arrested? She sounded…guilty. He took a guess. "Did you come?"

She swallowed audibly. "Yes, Sir."

He smothered a laugh. His dom brain said *bad sub*; his guy brain gloated that she'd gotten off thinking of him. "I see. While you're here, Summer, I'll take charge of those orgasms."

Chapter Eight

SUMMER HEARD THE amusement overlaying the steel in his voice, and relief ran through her. "Yes, Sir." Summer concentrated on not moving. Her pussy throbbed with the need to be touched, and all her senses focused on his finger resting on her outer folds.

"I have big hands, Summer, so open your legs until your feet are wider than the chair."

Heat seared her skin as she imagined those big hands on her. Touching her intimately. She put more weight on her arms and edged her feet out.

"Now bend your knees a little."

As she complied, her pussy opened wider, the puffy, wet folds peeling apart, exposing her core.

"That's right, honey." Virgil slid his hands between her legs, curved his palms under her ass cheeks, and lifted her. Leaning back, he lowered her until the backs of her thighs rested on the chair arms, and her feet dangled on the outside.

Her bottom bounced a few inches above his thighs, and she tightened her grip on his shoulders. He'd spread her so widely that she had no leverage to move. In fact, she probably couldn't get out of this position without help.

"That'll do," he said. Tilting his head, he licked one breast, then the other, starting the current sizzling up her center. He rested his thumbs in the creases between her hips and pelvis. So close to where she wanted him. *Oh God.* She quivered, needing his touch.

She closed her eyes and tried to regain her senses. To be fair. "It's your turn. You don't need to…to play with me or anything."

"You think?" A crease appeared in his cheek. Damn, when he looked at her like that, so amused and hot, she purely melted. "Summer. Whether I play or not is totally up to me. You don't get a vote."

He ran a finger around her slick entrance and pushed inside. His finger felt huge, wonderfully thick as he slid it slowly between her swollen tissues. "You're nice and wet for me, I see."

When he moved his hand away, she gritted her teeth. *Don't move, don't move.*

He unzipped his jeans. Commando. *Oh my.* She'd forgotten his size until his erection bobbed up and bounced against her pussy. Pleasure zinged up her spine.

She really, really wanted him inside her. Even more than getting off, her body cried out to be possessed. Filled. What would it feel like to be taken anally? As the thought shivered across her nerves, the muscles back there clenched.

After pulling a condom from his pocket, Virgil unpackaged something else—a pink circle with four nubby things around the sides.

"What is that?"

He gave her a narrow look. "Did I give you permission to speak?"

Oops.

He sheathed himself with the condom, then touched a side of the toy, and she heard buzzing. Another side. Increased buzzing. He worked the circle over his shaft. A cock ring *and* a vibrator?

She stared. If he was fully seated in her, those four sides of nubby humming things would press against her pussy, all around her entrance. Her legs flexed involuntarily, bouncing her bottom.

"That won't do." He put a hand under her butt, lifting her

slightly. "Move your legs forward, honey."

She edged her knees along the chair until her calves brushed against his upper arms, and her legs no long held her up. All her weight rested on his hand. With her grip on his shoulders barely keeping her balanced, and her legs over the chair arms, she could no longer lift or move her ass. He'd taken the last inch or so of control from her, and from the satisfied look in his eyes, he knew it.

Watching her closely, he fitted his cock to her entrance, and then lowered her. The big head pushed into her, and she opened around it. It felt so good.

But as she dropped farther, his thickness stretched her, more and more, until she hovered right at the edge of pain. She tried to lift up and couldn't. The knowledge of her helplessness swept through her, making her head spin. A whimper escaped.

He stopped immediately, although she could tell he wasn't completely in yet. She opened her eyes and met his intense gaze.

"You'll take all of me, but we can go slower." He lifted her bottom up and down in tiny increments, lubricating his shaft with her wetness. As the burning from being stretched subsided, she could feel the hum from the cock ring. God, he felt good.

More. She squirmed.

"Keep your hands on my shoulders," he warned.

Her fingers tightened. He chuckled. "And down you go." He pulled his hand out from under her.

She dropped the last few inches, gasping at the overwhelming fullness as he penetrated her completely. "Virgil!" Her insides clenched around him, over and over, and then the vibrations from the cock ring hit her clit, her labia and—holy heaven—another one pressed on her asshole.

He didn't move, keeping himself fully inside her, keeping her pussy resting right there on the vibrator.

"Oh my God." She started to pant as her clit tightened, hardened.

His laugh rumbled, and then his hands covered her breasts,

adding to the stimulation as he tugged on her nipples. Down below, the vibrations hit not just her clit, but every part of her pussy. His massive cock filled her completely. She lost herself in the overwhelming sensations. She clenched his shoulders as her insides started to tighten. The need to come built higher, an unfightable urge.

"You're damned gorgeous when you get all excited, but I don't want you getting off just yet." He gripped her hips and lifted her up. As he pulled her off his cock, the vibrations disappeared.

Her excitement slowed, leaving her clit aching and throbbing. When she whined, amusement joined the heat in his eyes.

Then he released her. Her pussy slid onto his shaft and pressed up against the buzzing ring. Her clit tightened, neared...

Before she could come, he yanked her up. Up until the head remained barely in her, then he let her drop. His cock stretched her, taking her breath, and she hit the vibrators. She squirmed, trying to get closer, more pressure.

Holding her hips in a bruising grip, he worked her pussy up and down on his cock, grinding his pelvis against her to maximize the vibrations. Each stroke increased her need, increased the pressure, until she teetered on the edge of an orgasm.

"You feel good," he said as her swollen clit pressed on the nubby vibrator. Her fingernails dug into his arms as her core tightened. Almost...

"I like that tight, hot cunt wrapped around me." He lifted her again, a second before she could come.

"Please. Oh God, please, Virgil." Too much. Her whole lower half pulsed with oversensitive nerves, needing more...more, more. When she tried to shake him, the sun lines at the corners of his eyes crinkled.

"More. Please." Was that her voice? Whining? Everything in her throbbed.

He didn't move for a moment that seemed to last forever.

"All right." He held her up with one hand, and the other hand slapped her bottom, damned hard. "Come now, Summer."

The stinging pain arrowed straight to her clit…and shoved her over. Pleasure fountained through her, exquisite sensations bubbling up against each nerve. Another wave hit, and she heard herself, her voice high and uncontrolled.

Growling his enjoyment, Virgil pumped her up and down, sending the orgasm rippling through all of her. As the sensations started to slow, he yanked her down, holding her there, completely filled and pressing on the cock ring.

The vibrations directly against her clit threw her into another spasm of pleasure. "Oooooh." Her hips wiggled uncontrollably in his grip.

His laugh came deep and rough. "Hang on, sweetie." His face pulled taut as he lifted her, then hammered into her, pistoning her body up and down. Her breasts bounced, and each thrust of his shaft sent more shuddering waves to engulf her until just the feeling of him inside her filled her world.

With a low groan, he pulled her against him so tightly she couldn't move. His cock jerked in her center and the sensation was…incredible.

Her head bowed. He'd cared enough to drive her into a mindless orgasm. And then…then he'd simply taken her for his own pleasure. Why did that give her the shivers—to be utterly used like that?

She sighed and squirmed as the vibrations from the cock ring started to irritate her swollen clit.

"Sensitive?" he murmured and lifted her up slightly with one hand until she no longer touched the toy. His eyes were heavy-lidded, his breathing rapid. He looked totally satisfied. *I did that.* The knowledge felt wonderful.

He caught her staring at him and smiled, then curved his free hand over her nape to pull her closer. His mouth took hers gently, a confusing contrast to the implacable grip on her neck.

"Mmm." She teased his lips, wondering how they could look so firm and feel so velvety.

He let her play, kissing her back, and then with a grunt, he used both hands to lift her straight up and off his cock. Still holding her up, he leaned forward, got his feet under him to rise. After turning, he put her down on the chair. "Stay here for a minute. I'll be right back."

The nonchalant display of his strength left her speechless. And wondering why all that strength seemed so barbarically sexy.

He returned, jeans zipped, and resumed his seat, this time snuggling her on his lap.

As she laid her head on his shoulder, she saw a couple watching from a few feet away. She stiffened, feeling…exposed, which didn't really make sense. She always played in public.

But this, tonight, had been different. She and Virgil had shared…more. Unsettled, she watched them walk away, feeling as if she finally understood Virgil's dislike of being on exhibit.

"Simon's sub says you're moving soon, out of San Francisco." His arm supported her as he ran his knuckles over her breasts, then lifted her chin up and frowned at her. "Tell me about that."

"Oh." Contentment filled her. He'd gotten off. He could just walk her to her cabin and leave. Instead, he started a conversation. The feel of his arm around her, his fingers against her face, and his focused attention bathed her with warmth. "Well. I realized I wanted more …"

She rambled, tucking her head back on his shoulder. Her limbs felt heavy, and she curled against him, feeling small and feminine. She could have easily fallen asleep, but he kept asking questions. About San Francisco. Her apartment. Her work.

As she talked, she realized again the emptiness of her life. "Anyway, I took the job in Gold Beach and start in a couple of weeks. My lease is up in four days, so I'm on a tight schedule."

He was silent. Too silent. She tried to sit up to look at his face—

"Gold Beach is in Oregon?" he asked.

"Um-hmm. On the coast."

"About an entire day's drive. Farther away than San Francisco." His voice was even. Emotionless. He sat quietly for a minute and then said, "I've got to get going. I work tomorrow morning."

"Oh." Disappointment seemed to dim the light in the room. "Okay." She rose reluctantly and started pulling on her clothes.

He stepped behind her and laced her corset with firm tugs. Chuckling, he turned her around. "Looks like I have my very own Bondage Barbie to play with and dress."

Her laugh turned into a gasp when he slid his fingers into the cups to adjust her left breast.

"What time do you leave?" he asked. He settled her other breast, his calloused fingers brushing against her nipple. As a hum ran through her system, she unconsciously leaned into his touch.

"Uh. What?" She looked up, caught his smile, and remembered his question. "Sunday around noon."

"I see." He kissed her, taking his time, his palm still curved around her breast. "I get off work at two tomorrow and then have a couple of errands to run. Do you want to test your courage and let me show you some of the area?"

"I—" Courage.

Before she could answer, he lifted her chin, forcing her to meet his eyes, his level, honest eyes. "No sex, no bondage. Just talking and maybe a kiss or two. You have my word."

Anxiety warred with the sheer desire to be with him. Desire won. *I will do this.* "Yes."

THE SUN SPARKLED on the light dusting of snow as Virgil pulled up to the lodge the next day. He spotted Summer waiting in front of her tiny cabin. Wearing a bright red parka, she looked like a very fuckable cardinal. His spirits rose.

He'd had a hell of a time sleeping last night. The bed had felt empty. He'd wanted her in his arms, wanted to breathe her peaches-and-vanilla scent, wanted to hear her lilting voice. Dammit, he hadn't known her long enough to miss her so much.

But he did. As she started down the path toward him, his anticipation rose. Fuck, she'd been beautiful, squirming on his shaft, jolting as the vibrations hit her clit. Hell of a toy, that cock ring.

Thank you, Angie. Of all the women he'd enjoyed, one had possessed the guts to show him how much fun toys could be. Shy creatures, females. They owned vibrators and dildos, liked using them, but hell would freeze over before they'd mention them to a man. These days, he'd insist on seeing a woman's collection—and might even pin her down while he used them. He snorted. Guess he'd been more of a dom than he'd realized.

Tapping his fingers on the steering wheel, he watched Summer cross the clearing and stifled his urge to escort her. Damn that fear of hers. Today, he intended to hear exactly what had happened to her. And then—he frowned. Tomorrow she'd leave for San Francisco to pack up and move.

His mood dropped like a boulder tumbling off a cliff. How could he pursue a relationship with her if it took two days just to drive there and back? And with the distance to the nearest airport, flight connections, and security precautions, taking a plane wasn't much better. His schedule didn't give him much time off—three day weekends were rare. Would she ever have the courage to visit him here without all her friends around?

As she approached the pickup, her blonde hair shone against the bright jacket, and her smile was contagious. He slid out to open the passenger side door for her.

"Thank you." She looked up at him, her blue eyes shining with pleasure…at seeing him.

He pulled her close, curving his hands under her lush ass, and took her mouth. Her lips were stiff, then soft and sweet. As he kissed her, he felt her body melt against his.

"I'd like to drag you into the lodge and fuck you speechless," he growled and watched her cheeks redden.

"Uh." Then she grinned. "We could do that."

He choked a laugh. How could he want her even more than he had five minutes ago? Leaning his forehead against hers, he said, "I can't skip my errands today. And maybe away from the lodge, I can talk to you without wondering how many times I can make you come."

"God, you're blunt," she muttered, making him laugh again.

"Let's go." He picked her up and set her into his truck, enjoying the simple pleasure of touching her. It would have to do for him…until tonight.

As they drove up the mountain, she sat forward, watching everything, her interest as appealing as hell. He slowed off and on, pointing out a herd of deer, the various cabins that normally couldn't be seen from the road, then a cardinal that matched her jacket.

At the end of a rutted road, he parked in front of Laurette Mann's stone and log home. "Ms. Laurette, it's Virgil," he called as he swung out of the truck. Not waiting for his help, Summer jumped out. As she petted the ancient gray cat, Virgil grabbed the box of groceries from the pickup bed.

The elderly widow opened the door, her cheeks pink with excitement. "Virgil, come in, dear. I have tea on."

He stepped aside to let Summer precede him into the living room. "Ms. Laurette, this is Summer. She's visiting from San Francisco. Summer, Ms. Laurette and her husband designed and built this place—oh, about thirty years ago."

Summer turned in a circle, eyes wide. "It's beautiful," she said sincerely.

"Why, thank you." Laurette beamed at her. "Let me show you around."

Perfect. "I'll tuck your groceries away and join you in a minute." And Laurette wouldn't argue about the extras he'd added to her order.

Chapter Nine

AFTER A PLEASANT tea with Laurette, Virgil took a service road deep into the forest, parking at one of his favorite spots. "We're here." Near the half-frozen creek, he spread a thick pad and blanket on a bare patch of ground.

Frowning, Summer followed with the basket. "It's the dead of winter, Virgil. Not picnic season."

Damn, she was pretty. He sat and pulled her down, then wrapped a blanket around them to keep in their body heat. And it made a good excuse to have her soft curves pressed against his. He handed her a fat ham sandwich from the basket and a thermos of tomato soup.

"Eat, sweetheart." He kissed her cheek before starting on his own.

"You know, Midwesterners are smart enough to save picnics for summertime." Still looking a little bemused, she took a bite of the sandwich.

"Only because they're too wimpy to stand the cold."

Her elbow jabbed his ribs in reprisal, and he barked a laugh.

Ignoring him, she smiled at the snowy branches of the pines and tilted her head to listen to the cheerful gurgle of the creek. "It's sure beautiful here." She didn't say anything else, didn't try to fill the silence with empty conversation. Along with the warmth from her body, contentment seeped into him. They weren't immersed in any sex-charged atmosphere now, and he still liked being with her more than anyone else he'd ever known.

During the afternoon, he'd gotten a better handle on her personality. In the truck she'd listed off things, like shower rails and grab bars, that he and his brothers could install to keep Laurette safe. And if he hadn't promised to follow through, she'd undoubtedly dig up the supplies and return on her own. A warm, caring—and determined—woman.

As she leaned against his shoulder, he knew he'd be happy just sitting with her...forever.

A rustling sounded in the undergrowth. He whispered, "Shhhh." Twilight arrived early in the winter mountains, and he'd deliberately chosen this site. He pointed and watched her eyes widen as three deer came down to the stream to drink.

When they'd finished and bounded up the slope, she sighed. "They're beautiful. There's good hiking around Gold Beach, they said. I'd like to get into the forests more often."

Dammit, how the hell could he stand having her live so far away? He cleared his throat. "You going to get homesick for San Francisco?"

"A bit. Not for the city, but for my friends and their families."

"Ah." Yes, she was a sociable person. He ran a hand down her hair, playing with the silky strands. A whiff of vanilla made him want to open her clothes and nuzzle her skin. "Where's your own family?"

"Nebraska. My brother and mom are still on the farm. I love them, but I wanted to see more of the world."

"A farm to San Francisco? That's a jump." He eyed her. "You got a job and moved?"

"Unfortunately, no." She gave a short...bitter...laugh. "Innocent me—I fell for a guy visiting Nebraska, and he asked me to come here and live with him."

"Something went wrong?"

"The usual. He discovered he liked someone better and showed me the door." She scowled at her hands. "God, I was stupid."

"Risking something for love isn't stupid, honey." Her unhappy expression squeezed his chest and pissed him off. A shame the guy wasn't around to have his face rearranged. "What happened after you broke up?"

"Mom and Andy were strapped for money at the time, so I was stuck with no friends and no job. I didn't have my RN license for California yet. I finally got work as a waitress. It was just one of those life lessons in survival." Her voice sounded light, but he saw the shadows in her eyes.

He pulled her closer, although there was no protecting someone from her past.

After a second, she shrugged and smiled slightly. "Then again, I'd gotten out of Nebraska to San Francisco. I'd never have dreamed of moving so far on my own. There's always a bright side."

"And you're the type who'd find it." He tipped her face up and kissed her. Everything he learned seemed to slide her farther into his heart. A kiss only, he reminded himself. More would frighten her. Time to find out why.

SHE'D BE HAPPY kissing him forever, Summer decided.

He nipped her lower lip and pulled back. "Now tell me about the incident Simon mentioned." His voice had deepened and roughened—not a request, but an order.

Her breath fled. "That—"

"Summer, I need to know what happened. Not only because you mean something to me"—he kissed her palm—"but also because I'm your dom." His eyes pinned her. "Now tell me."

He was right…and she didn't want to think about it, especially now in the sweetness of the afternoon with him.

He waited, as immovable as the mountains around them.

"Fine." She tried to pull her hand back…unsuccessfully. No retreat, physical or emotional. "I'd met a dom at Dark Haven. The party at Simon's house was our first date outside of the club." God, she'd acted so recklessly.

"Sounds like it should have been safe," he said mildly, his tone nonjudgmental.

"I'm only grateful I didn't go to his apartment instead." She stared at her hand, enclosed within his warm fingers. "When we arrived, he wanted a private spot to play." She didn't think about the similarity to Virgil's complaint until she felt his fingers tighten. *Oh God.* An apology would make it worse, so she forged on. "He found an isolated place under the stairs and chained me to a post there. And gagged me."

She swallowed against the memory of the taste of the rubber ball-gag. *Drool running down my chin, so humiliating. Choking on the gag.* She'd shaken her head, used her safe word. He'd understood her. Ignored her. *The blooming of fear. Horror.*

"Go on." Virgil brought her back.

"He used a cane." Each strike had sent bladelike pain all the way to the bone. "He heard me use my safe word, over and over, but the gag kept anyone else from hearing me." *Agonizing blow after blow, as if my skin was being sliced to pieces.* The whole world red with pain. She screamed, pulled at the restraints, tearing her wrists, an animal, mindless. "He laughed…and kept hitting me."

Silence.

She looked up. He'd closed his eyes, his face like stone. "Virgil?" His eyes opened, so green and cold with anger that she flinched.

She saw his effort to calm, to force his muscles to relax before he said quietly, "I'm sorry, baby, but the thought of you hurt and helpless makes me…unhappy." He put his arm around her, pulling her close. "So what happened?"

His arm was heavy. Warm. His controlled strength pushed her memories back, clearing a space for thoughts. "Rona, Simon's sub, happened. She walked past and realized I was saying 'red.' Her yelling brought Simon and everyone else." She rubbed her head against his chest. "The Hunt brothers were there too."

"Logan, Jake, *and* Simon?" The almost palpable vibration of his anger diminished. "Is the son-of-a-bitch dom still alive?"

She tried to laugh through the tightness of her throat. "I found out yesterday Simon broke his nose, and the Hunts walloped him before they tossed him out."

"Not nearly enough," Virgil muttered. "How badly beat up were you?"

Waves of pain filling her until even the air seemed edged in fire. She shuddered and yanked herself from the memory. Thank God the post had protected her front. "I hurt for a while," she said lightly.

"Don't hand me bullshit, Summer. If I ask, I want a truthful answer."

"Fine then, I hurt like hell," she snapped. "I had welts pretty much everywhere. Bruises over the bones, places where my skin had split, and I peed blood for two days."

"Jesus." He yanked her onto his lap, holding her so tightly her ribs creaked. "No wonder you have problems. You have a couple scars on your back. Are they…?"

"Yeah." He'd seen them. Hadn't said anything. "A friend—another nurse—took me home with her. I had good care."

"I'm surprised you even considered BDSM after that." The respect in his voice was heartening.

She rubbed her cheek on his chest. "I hadn't planned to, but Simon dragged me back."

Virgil snarled under his breath, and she realized her error. *Dragged.* "No, I said that wrong. Rona's in admin at my hospital, and after I returned to work, she recognized me from the party. One day, Simon showed up, bought me coffee in the cafeteria, and quizzed me about my experience, what I wanted, what I'd liked. I guess he could tell I…" *Want it. Need it.* "Anyway, he and Rona talked me into going back with them. They babysat me. He kept introducing me to experienced doms, but they scared me. I preferred...easier ones."

"I understand." His chin rested on the top of her head. "I'm glad I came along when you were finally ready, baby," he said.

She hesitated, but his warmth somehow opened her like a springtime flower. "I don't think I'd have ever been ready," she admitted. "I don't know why, but I trust you. Even when you scare me."

"Mmm." His arms tightened. "Then we'll go on from here."

▲

NIGHT HAD FALLEN by the time they got back to the lodge. On the porch, Summer turned to say good night and tripped over Logan's scarred-up dog that sprawled in front of the door. Sitting beside him, a giant cat watched with unblinking eyes.

"Have you met Thor and Mufasa, Summer?" Virgil performed the introductions with as much formality as he had with Laurette.

After the dog lifted a paw for her to shake, the cat padded over.

"You really are a beauty, even if you're huge," Summer said and offered her finger.

Mufasa sniffed the digit carefully, then politely nudged it with her cheek. *Accepted. You may pet me.*

Grinning, Summer complied. The tabby-colored hair was soft and thick with the winter's undercoat. How had she gone so long without an animal to love? "I want a dog."

"Why not have one?" Virgil gave Thor a full-body scratch that had the dog shivering in delight.

"I could barely afford my tiny apartment, definitely not one allowing pets. Maybe I can get one once I'm settled." Longing filled her heart. A dog to love. Something that needed her.

"I hope you do." Virgil bent to give her a warm kiss. "I'll get back here by nine. Be in the lodge, dressed and ready to play." He drew his finger slowly along her jaw. "I'm looking forward to having my hands on your body again. To hear the sounds you make when I suck your nipples. To feel you coming around my cock."

At his words and the flammable look in his eyes, her insides melted like ice under a hot sun.

The corner of his mouth turned up with satisfaction. He set something in her hand—a package and a packet of lube. "This is to prepare that little asshole of yours. Put it in now and remove it before you come to the lodge."

She frowned at the anal plug. He'd touch her there, hold her hips as he pushed into her. He'd hurt her—and please her. She shivered as he held her gaze. Self-assured. Firm. She nodded, her mouth too dry to form a word.

"That's my girl," he said so softly it was like a brush of wind against her heart.

Chapter Ten

A LITTLE BEFORE nine, Summer shrugged out of her coat and left her boots in the row by the door. She grinned at the music Logan had selected to start off the night. The snapping whip in Lambert's *For Your Entertainment* was echoed by a real one farther down the room. In the glow of wall sconces and firelight, Doms and subs set up for their play, laying out toys to use, checking tools and restraints. Nearby, a naked sub stood patiently while her dom wrapped her in rope for a suspension scene.

Off to one side, Logan had his arm around Rebecca, supervising. He gave Summer a once-over. "Very sexy, sugar."

She smiled, heartened by his compliment and Rebecca's subtle thumbs-up. Maybe she hadn't wasted her time with an hour of primping. She'd copied MaryAnn and braided a few locks of hair, adding in dark blue beads that matched her bustier and leather skirt. She'd gone heavier with her makeup, so her eyes looked bigger. With luck, her glossy lipstick would have Virgil demanding a blowjob.

She'd like to give him a blowjob. *Oh yeah.* Two nights now and she still hadn't had a chance to play with his cock. Maybe start by running her tongue over the head. Just as a tease. Maybe he'd wrap her hair around his hand and—

The door opened to a blast of frigid air and swirling snow-flakes, and a bear-sized man stepped in. *Virgil.* Every nerve in her body turned happy handsprings.

He tossed his coat in the heap on a couch and stomped the snow off. Typical BDSM attire of black jeans and boots. But what kind of dom wore a flannel shirt, even if it was black? She shook her head. The man sure did things his own way.

His gaze moved down her body, pausing on her breasts, her thighs and legs, and fire lit his eyes, igniting a matching flame inside her. He tilted his head. "You are the sexiest, prettiest woman I've seen in just about forever."

The sincerity in his voice staggered her. Sure, she'd thought she looked good, but somehow when he said it, the impact was entirely different. "Thank you, Sir."

Virgil nodded at Logan, then set an arm over her shoulder. "Let's get some water, and we'll talk about tonight."

Halfway to the kitchen, Simon called Virgil over to the fireplace. "Rona wants to ski while we're here. Can you recommend a place?"

"A couple of them are good. Do you have a pen?" Virgil asked.

Looked like they'd be at it for a few minutes. "I'll get the water and come back," Summer said.

"Thank you, sweetie." Virgil squeezed her arm gratefully. "We won't talk long, I promise."

She entered the kitchen, feeling appreciated. And sexy.

A hefty, potbellied man stood by the counter. "Hey there, hottie," he said with a leer and waggled his beer at her.

Maybe there were times sexy wasn't so good. "Hi." She gave him a politely cool smile.

Stepping past him to get to the refrigerator, she noticed that instead of the popular cop or military fetwear, he wore a gas company uniform. How odd.

When he took a long pull of the beer, she frowned. Dark Haven had strict rules about no alcohol before BDSM play. "Quite a party," he said, jerking his chin at the doorway.

"Uh-huh." She started to pull open the refrigerator door.

She felt a hand run down her butt to between her legs. Dammit! She spun around and glared at him.

He snorted. "Don't give me that pure and innocent expression. I saw what's going on in there. One big orgy. So we're going to have one out here, just you and me." His gaze traveled down her body like a wash of slime.

What a creep. "Not interested."

His face reddened, his expression changing until it had nothing to do with domination and everything to do with violence and rape. "Cunt. No cunt talks to me that way." His words echoed in the kitchen…the very empty kitchen.

Uneasiness skittered across her nerves as she realized he had her cornered between the massive table and the wall of appliances.

She retreated a step and stopped. Jaw tight, she shook off the encroaching panic. *I'm not restrained, not gagged. Not helpless.* Straightening her back, she gave him a steady stare. "Leave now, before this goes any further."

He rubbed his crotch, his piggy eyes on her. "You're giving it away free; I'm going to get me some snatch too." She could smell the alcohol on his breath.

A drunk. That's very bad. Her heart began to hammer against her tightening chest. Summer planted her feet, her hands fisting. Then, not being stupid, she yelled, "Help!"

"Fucking bitch!" He grabbed at her.

Smothering a squeak, she knocked his arm aside. With all her strength, she punched him in the jaw. Pain burst in her knuckles.

He staggered back—right into Virgil. Virgil stepped in front of him, set a hand on his chest, and casually shoved. The creep hit the refrigerator door with a horrible thump, and his eyes went unfocused.

Virgil studied Summer for a moment, then gave her a fleeting smile that did nothing to warm the ice in his eyes.

Well. Talk about a timely rescue. She realized her hands were still fisted and uncurled her fingers.

"Not a good plan, buddy." Virgil's voice was mild. "Supposedly the last poor fucker here who tried rape was given to the femdommes who whipped all the skin off his back…and his dick."

It took a minute for the man to figure it out. Then his face paled. "Hey, don't—nothin' happened." He gave Summer a pleading look. "I got carried away."

He edged sideways to avoid Virgil. Once free, he staggered toward the back door. Catching sight of Logan and Simon in the doorway, he shrank another inch and sped up.

Logan's face looked like stone when he glanced at Summer. "I'm sorry, sugar. His gas truck broke down. Since the tow truck can't get out here until morning, I gave him a cabin. He wasn't supposed to leave it."

Her throat was almost too dry for the words to get past. "Not your fault he didn't obey." She hugged herself, feeling as if her bones were covered in ice.

"Summer." Virgil's deep voice drew her gaze. He held out his hand. She hesitated only a second, then flew into his arms.

He enclosed her in safety and warmth, rocking her gently. "Good punch, slugger," he said against her ear. "You okay?"

She nodded, knowing the way she'd attached herself to his waist might tell him differently. He didn't call her on it, just held her firmly. His flannel shirt felt soft under her cheek, with a homelike scent of laundry detergent.

Around her, the men talked quietly. Logan growled that he'd make sure the man never worked anywhere around Yosemite again, then started grumbling about Virgil's tall tale. "Whip-cracking dommes?"

Virgil chuckled. "Gullible bastard believed it."

"I rather enjoyed the story," Simon said. "I was afraid you'd mop the floor with him instead of terrifying him with femdommes."

Virgil shrugged. "Summer nailed him good, I'd say. And I've had my fill of violence. I'll bust somebody's chops if that's what it takes, but there's usually a better choice."

Summer lifted her head and met Simon's gaze. He smiled slightly, and she realized he was still trying to help her.

But she'd started to think she knew Virgil Masterson. She rubbed her cheek against his hard chest, then pulled back. "How'd you get to the kitchen so fast?"

"I was almost here. I don't like leaving you alone for long, not at this kind of party." He ran a finger across her jaw.

"Oh." Like having her own guardian angel. Why did she find that so comforting? "Thanks for the protection."

"Part of the job description," he murmured.

She tilted her head. "Which job?"

His eyes crinkled. "All of them, baby. All of them." From the wry humor in his smile, he meant it too. "Let me grab some water, and we'll find a place to talk a bit."

He was willing to play here even when he didn't want to…just because she was a coward. How could she think he'd ever hurt her? And how long would she let Dirk sabotage her life? "Actually"—all the air seemed to have been sucked out of the room, so she took a second to find some—"I'd just as soon talk at your place, if it's still an option."

She'd surprised him. His eyes sharpened, and he studied her face for a long, long moment. Then his gaze flickered over her shoulders, her hands. A cop's stare. A dom's assessment. Finally he nodded with a fleeting smile. "It's definitely an option. Do you want to grab anything from your cabin, or should I tuck you in the truck while you still have the courage?"

Oh. Very good point. "Let's make a run for it."

His growly laugh filled the room. "Then that's what we'll do."

WHEN VIRGIL TURNED the truck down a tiny road, Summer worked on controlling her breathing. Almost there. The dirt road widened into a small open valley. A barn and stockades sat off to the right, and farther out, snowy pastures glowed in the moonlight. The headlights showed the dark forest flowing up the mountain on the left and then illumined a massive two-story log house.

He took her in through a side door. After removing her boots, he led the way up the stairs and opened one of the two doors, flipping on the light.

She smiled at his warm and cozy living room. Cushy chairs of brown and tan plaid flanked a huge dark green sofa. A newspaper lay discarded on a leather ottoman. Across the room, an open door revealed a large bedroom. *Well, damn.* The man had himself a second floor suite that was as big as her apartment.

As he went to hang her coat up, she curled and uncurled her toes in the thick brown carpet. *I'm not scared. Uh-uh.*

"I'll get a fire lit." He set his toy bag down on a chair next to the couch and knelt in front of a stone fireplace. A herd of carved horses galloped across the mantel. Paperbacks stuffed the built-in bookcases. He liked to read. She hadn't known.

What else don't I know? she wondered with an ugly tinge of worry.

On her right was a flat-screen TV with theater system and a wealth of movies in more shelves. Creamy-colored walls lightened the room and showcased Remington prints. She smiled, remembering his so-worn-looking western clothing in Dark Haven. It definitely hadn't been a costume.

After closing the glass fireplace door, he flicked off the overhead lights so the only illumination came from firelight. He picked up a remote and punched something in, and the low tones of Enya filled the room.

Setting the scene. Her skin chilled.

"Summer." He held out his hand.

She crossed the room, wishing she wore jeans and a flannel shirt instead of fetwear.

"Can I get you something to drink?"

She shook her head, mouth dry.

"All nerves, aren't you," he said softly. His hands curled around her upper arms. He pulled her up on tiptoes as he kissed her, no longer sweetly but with pent-up desire, demanding a response as he possessed her mouth. Her senses whirled like fallen leaves in a storm.

When he finally released her, she wanted him with every fiber in her being.

"There now, that's the look I like to see on your face." His voice had turned husky; his golden-brown eyes were filled with heat.

She swallowed and rubbed her damp hands on her skirt.

The sun lines at the corners of his eyes crinkled. "You know, every time you put on these sexy clothes, all I can think about is getting you out of them." He undid the hooks on her bustier. Despite the cold outside, his hands were warm. His calloused fingers scraped lightly over her nipples, teasing them into hard peaks.

She wanted—needed—to touch him, and she ran her palms up his forearms. The corded tendons and muscles under the light brown hair made her clench inside. He was so strong.

He tossed her bustier onto a chair, her leather skirt followed, and she stood naked in the center of the room. Exposed and vulnerable. Deep in her belly, excitement flickered to life.

When she shivered despite the heat under her skin, he set her on the padded arm of the couch and dragged it closer to the fireplace.

She could feel the warmth radiating from the blazing fire, hear the muted pops of the burning wood. What was there about a fire that satisfied a primitive need? She shook her head. Probably the same one that craved a man's strength.

When Virgil stroked her hair, she looked up and frowned. "You're still dressed."

"Yep." He smiled and pushed her over backward.

"Hey!" Her shoulders hit the cushions, but he'd held on to her hips, so her bottom remained up high on the arm of the couch. Her legs dangled over the side. She struggled to sit up.

He jerked her hips, flattening her again. "Stay right there, Summer." His eyes narrowed. "If you don't move, I won't restrain you."

Her thumping heart dented the inside of her ribs.

"Do you understand, little sub?" he asked softly. "I want a polite answer."

When he used that authoritative tone… The flood of excitement swept her willpower away. "Yes, Sir."

"Good. Put your arms over your head."

She did, then frowned. With her butt up so high, she couldn't move without using her arms.

"Very nice." He set her left foot on the tall back cushions, exposing the apex of her thighs. She saw him smile and realized he'd positioned the couch so the firelight glowed right on her pussy. The warmth from the fire, from his body, bathed her legs.

His finger traced down her lower stomach, over her mound to between her legs. "It's damned sexy how you're always nice and wet for me," he rumbled in approval. His fingers opened her more, and he ran a finger around her entrance to over her clit. Her hips jolted upward.

"Virgil." How could he make her feel so exposed and so aroused at the same time. She moved her leg down.

"Mmmm?" Without even looking, he pinned her leg against the back cushions with his right side, keeping her spread open. He pushed her other leg outward, so she ended up wider than before.

He bent, and his lips touched the place just below her mound where her folds started.

Too far from her clit, yet she almost groaned with the way everything tightened. Swelled.

He teased the spot, his tongue so hot and wet. She tried to lift her hips up to him, and he flattened her butt on the arm of the couch. "If you move again, I'll spank you first. And then start over."

Oh God.

With his tongue, he delicately traced circles around her core until her hands fisted. "Virgil, I can't..."

His eyes had never left her face, and she realized the position let him watch her reactions to everything he did with his mouth. He lifted his head, and his breath brushed over her sensitized skin. "No, you can't do a thing." He smiled slightly, then licked upward from her entrance and over the ball of nerves, his hands tightening on her hips when she jerked uncontrollably.

God, with every touch of his tongue, her clit swelled until it felt ten times larger than normal. Tight and hot. "I need more. Sir. I want you inside me."

"You can have this for now, baby." He reached into his bag, and she heard a slight buzz. Then he slowly pushed something between her puffy tissues. Long and thin, it vibrated in her, ratcheting up her arousal.

"Not quite there. Need more curve," he said, and removed the device. A click and when he put it back in, the vibrations hit right on the oh-so-sensitive spot at her core. *Oh God, yes.* It felt as if her nerves had expanded inward, so when he rocked the toy, the buzzing hit her clit from the inside. Her hands fisted as her need shot into urgency.

"Mmm, that's the right spot," he murmured.

She clenched and moaned, tilting up her hips until he set his forearm across her pelvis, pinning her down—and his ruthless control somehow shot the pressure to the boiling point.

The slow rocking and the deep-seated vibrations drove her upward. She was going to die. And then he took her clit between his lips and sucked, each strong pull of his mouth coinciding with his pushing the vibrator onto that...spot inside. Her hips strained against his arm as every nerve tightened, and she teetered at the brink, unable to even breathe, as if the universe had stopped.

He sucked harder, his tongue swirled roughly over her clit, and her senses exploded into engulfing pleasure, sweeping everything before it in a tornado of sensation, flattening every thought in its path until only feeling remained.

When her body went limp, when her eyes focused again, she realized the room had definitely warmed up. Her heart still hammered so hard—God, she could have had a heart attack. She wet her lips. "That was…wonderful."

"Mmm, it was fun."

Fun? She'd almost *died*, and he thought it was just fun?

He removed the toy and ran his hands over her thighs before kissing each one. "You have such soft skin," he murmured.

She sighed like a kitten in a basketful of wool, all warm and cozy.

His smile flashed. "Don't get comfortable, slugger. We're not done yet." He took her hands and pulled her up to stand by the couch. "Kneel, please. I want those shiny lips of yours around my cock."

Chapter Eleven

AS VIRGIL GAVE the order, he realized they'd never discussed blowjobs. Maybe this was too much for—

Delight flashed in her eyes. "*Yes, Sir.*" She dropped to her knees. After putting a hand on his waistband, she glanced up as if to make sure she did what he wanted, then unzipped and freed him from his jeans. The firelight flickered over her hair, like a pale waterfall down her back. Dark beads swung from the tiny braids.

She curled her fingers around the base of his shaft, her hand so small her thumb didn't meet her fingers. Her lips closed over the head, and he tensed, anticipating the heat. She gave him a wicked look and instead ran her tongue up his length, teasing the winding veins and the dent under the head.

He muffled a groan and forced himself to gently stroke her silky hair. After licking up the precum, she swirled her hot little tongue over and around the head. Fuck, maybe this wasn't the best idea. If he got any harder, the skin on his cock would rip apart. "Enough teasing, brat," he muttered and fisted his hand in her hair.

She giggled. Hell, she sounded cute—and delighted she could threaten his control. Although he saw her ass wiggle as if the idea of being punished appealed to her, she obeyed. She closed her mouth around him, rubbing her tongue down the underside as her lips slid almost to the base. Up and down. Slowly.

Dammit. He pulled her hair, pushing his hips forward, going

deeper, faster. Her mouth tightened as she sucked forcefully. Pulling back, she circled the head with her tongue and took him in so fast that his eyes almost rolled back. She worked her free hand into his jeans to fondle his balls. The pressure at the bottom of his spine built.

With a hum that vibrated through his cock, she took him deeper until he hit the back of her throat. "Jesus, you're going to kill me." His leg muscles tightened as he fought for control. Her glossy lips left shiny trails on his shaft. Hot, wet, the suction unbelievable.

No.

"Stop, sweetheart." He gripped her shoulders and moved her back, although he fucking well wanted to grab her hair and pump himself in and out of that devastatingly soft mouth. He caressed her face, wiping the saliva from her cheek. "You are frighteningly good at that."

"But you want me to stop?" Her big eyes held heat and confusion.

"I'm going to come in a different place tonight."

Although a tiny tremor ran through her, she didn't scream and flee. Progress.

Without giving her time to get nervous, he set her on the leather ottoman, positioning her on forearms and knees. He wound two scarves from the toy bag around her wrists, tying them to the ottoman legs.

Her breathing hitched, and the muscles in her shoulders tensed.

Go slow, Masterson. He knelt in front of her and lifted her face, forcing her to look at him. "Summer, breathe."

Wide blue eyes met his, and her obvious trust squeezed his heart. She inhaled slowly and nodded.

He studied her for another minute, running his thumb over her chin. Not shaking, hands open, eyes focused. "Good." He kissed her lightly and nibbled the tempting lower lip before whispering, "Don't tell Simon, since I'm probably breaking some dominant rule, but the scarves are loose enough you can escape if you have to."

She blinked in surprise, pulled up on her right hand, then whispered back, "Thank you."

He stroked her cheek. "Just remember I'll be disappointed if you do take them off. It will please me if you stay put, honey."

When she looked at him, no panic showed, only the expression he'd seen a time or two. Determination and joy. She wanted to please him. It went both ways—he hoped to take her on the finest journey of her submissive life. "That's my girl." *And you are, whether you know it or not.*

He looped scarves around her knees, securing them to the sides of the ottoman so her legs were spread wide. He'd never used his ottoman like this before, but it damned well seemed as if someone had designed it for bondage.

Keeping his touch easy, he slid his hand over her pussy. Very wet and slick, and as he fingered her clit, it hardened. She gave a small moan. There would be more moans before he finished tonight.

He pinched the swollen nub of nerves lightly, and she jumped, pulling at the scarves. Then she recalled her instructions and quieted, but her breathing increased. She grew wetter, obviously turned on by restraints, verbal or physical.

Submissive. And mine. As he teased the hood of her clit, he reminded her, "Your safe word is *safe word*, Summer." He ran his hand over her soft, round bottom, warming the skin, waking the nerves. "I'm going to take your ass, honey. I'll go slow, but I will be in you before we're done. And you will come for me while I'm inside you."

SUMMER FELT VIRGIL'S calloused hand rubbing her bottom. His deep, firm voice held no doubts of what would happen, and she shivered. She bit her lips and waited, every nerve on her skin alive and tingling.

When he sheathed himself with a condom, her breathing

hitched. She shut her eyes. *I don't want to see any more.*

A second later, he pulled her buttocks apart, and cold lube drizzled onto her asshole, making her squeak. His finger pressed against her, uncomfortable for a second, then breached the muscle and slid in.

Her fingernails dug into the ottoman at the impossible feelings shooting through her.

"You're more relaxed," he murmured. "You used the plug. Good girl."

The momentary rush of pleasure from his words was followed by a mewl of surprise as his second finger joined the first. *Ohhhh.* Unfamiliar sensations ran through her, discomfort mingling with excitement. He was really going to do this. *Oh God.*

He stroked her clit with his free hand, his fingers in her ass moved slowly in and out, and the combination started to push her upward to total arousal.

After a minute, he pulled out, and she felt his heavy cock press on her asshole. The head slid slickly over her puckered rim. "Push back against me, Summer."

She bit her lip, hands clenching into fists, and tried to comply. He mercilessly gripped her hip, keeping her from moving away, as he steadily pushed in.

"Oh God," she whimpered, as the ring of muscle stretched and burned. Her body shook uncontrollably.

And then with a pop, the head of his cock was in. He didn't move as she panted. Trapped. Impaled. Hurting.

"You're still tight," he said. "Breathe, honey. Deep breath."

The pressure eased as her body adjusted. He rubbed her bottom, and more cold liquid trickled between her buttocks. More lube. A second later, he pressed forward, in and out in tiny increments, working deeper, gradually stretching her.

Her back hole felt on fire, as if he'd grown much, much bigger than before—huge—the size of a house. She moaned as he advanced farther and farther. Eons later, the warm skin and coarse hair on his thighs finally pressed on her buttocks. "There we go, baby. All in."

She felt totally penetrated, pinned by his hard cock inside her. Her head whirled as she pulled on her restraints, struggled against his hands, knowing she couldn't go anywhere, knowing he'd taken her most private place. The rush of heat shook her, scared her. He had all the control, she had none.

He didn't move. "Easy, baby. Shhh."

After a minute, she stilled, gasping for air. Exhausted.

He slid out a little and back in.

It didn't feel good—it hurt. She whined, trying not to use her safe word. Wanting to please him. Wanting it to stop.

A hum sounded, and he pressed something soft against her clit. A vibrator. She stiffened with surprise, reflexively started to pull away.

With a huff of amusement, he yanked her back, embedding him even deeper, and she yelped.

Intense vibrations surged into her throbbing clit and collided with the burning, stretching pain from her ass. Not comfortable or sweet but strange and overwhelming.

"You're a good girl," he said, his voice low and rough. He wrapped straps around her thighs, securing the vibrator against her clit. Then his powerful hands gripped her hips, and he pulled back, slow at first. He added even more lube until his shaft grew slick.

He'd filled her completely, then withdrew, then pushed in again. The friction of his cock against the wealth of sensitive nerves was incredible. She shook, unable to move, to think, to do anything except suffer the painful, wonderful, thrilling feel of him sliding in and out, and the demanding vibrations against her clit. The pressure, the need to come, coiled her insides with urgency, until she teetered on the edge of orgasm.

And stayed there forever. Her body froze. She panted for air. "Oh God, oh God, oh God, I can't."

He rumbled a laugh and reached around her to jam the vibrator against her clit as he shoved his cock deeper.

She broke completely, as everything inside her—everything—exploded into brutal, terrifying waves of pleasure. The uncontrollable sensations racked her body, and a high scream tore out of her. His hard hands controlled her bucking as he hammered into her, pushing her deeper into the overwhelming lake of sensation.

HE COULDN'T LAST, Virgil knew, not with her softness all around his cock and the tight ring of muscle circling the base. More…a little more.

And then the muscles of his legs turned rigid. The pressure at the base of his spine expanded, clenching his balls until they drew up tight against his groin, and a second later, fiery pleasure blasted into his cock. His release jerked up through his shaft and shot out in heart-stopping spasms.

He thrust hard, driving as deep as he could, until his eyes tried to roll back in his head from sheer pleasure.

Sweat trickled down the hollow of his back as he hauled in a long breath. He'd happily have stood there forever, enjoying the glory of being inside her, but she'd started to wilt.

He flicked the thigh straps open, and the vibrator dropped away. She shuddered. Her head drooped, only the scarves keeping her from flattening into a pancake on the ottoman. "Sweetie, hold on a minute longer," he said, running his hands over her smooth back.

His withdrawal made her moan, and he grinned.

After removing the condom, he cleaned her off with baby wipes. Her pussy reacted to the touch of the cool cloth with small spasms that made him want to fuck her again. And again and again.

Instead, he untied her. Lifting her in his arms, he shoved a chair closer to the fire and settled into it. She curled up in his lap, her head against his chest. She looked confused. Lost. Little tremors shook her.

"Pretty Summer. You were very brave." He stroked her, warming her skin with his hands, holding her firmly. Grounding her. He kissed her cheek, wanting nothing more than to hold her, keep her in his life forever. "God, I love you."

"Mmm." She lifted her hand and touched his jaw, then stiffened. "Huh?"

"You heard me." He nuzzled her hair. Would he ever smell vanilla again without getting an erection? "I learned a harsh lesson this year—that I should never assume someone knows how I feel." His cousin Kallie had suffered, and he bore part of the blame. He'd bear the guilt to his grave. He'd not hesitate to speak again. "You'll never have to guess what I feel for you. I love you, Summer."

Her lips opened…then closed tightly. She shook her head. "No, no you don't. It's just because we had sex. We barely met. You can't think you l-love me."

His hopes started to disappear under a cold mudslide of disappointment, and then his jaw tightened. She did have a point. They didn't know each other well, which also meant she had no idea how fucking stubborn he could be.

"Can't I?" He rubbed his cheek against hers. "I haven't learned everything about your past, but I know you, baby. How you react when you're frightened or you want something, how much it means to you to help people, what you do when you get angry." His lips curved as he remembered her punching the bastard. He tilted her chin up, forcing her to meet his eyes. "I understand how much you need me, how much you care."

"I…" Her voice shook. "It's too soon, Virgil."

Now look at that—she hadn't denied either the need or the caring. "You think?"

"Okay, maybe I…care. That doesn't matter." She turned her face away. "I don't see any way this could work for us."

The exhilaration sheered through him, and it took a minute to hear the second part. "You don't want to continue what we started?"

Her tear-filled eyes were like a lake reflecting the blue sky. "I do," she whispered. "But…but, Virgil, there's nothing for me here. I have a career that I can't abandon. And I won't be dependent on someone, not even you."

He took a long, slow breath. He shouldn't push her. But her plans would put her so far away. He played with the silky hair spilling over her breasts. "Do you want me to move to Gold Beach with you?"

She stared at him. "You can't leave here. You have people who depend on you. A job. Your mountain. I… You mustn't."

"Mmmmh." *Back off, Masterson.* He tightened his arms around her like he could force her to stay. Not happening.

He considered for a second how he'd feel about not having a job, being dependent on her. *Fuck no.* Especially at this point in their relationship. "I think we can figure something out, sweetheart."

"I want… If only…" She blew out an exasperated huff. "You don't even have a hospital here."

She wanted to stay. Hope flickered like a candle and died. No hospital. Only one doctor in town—in the whole area within decent driving distance—and hell would freeze over before Abe'd hire a nurse. His mouth tightened.

Her hand sliding up his chest distracted him. She tried to smile for him. "So since we don't have much time, how about some shower sex?"

A distraction? Good choice. He rose with her still in his arms. "We can do that."

He made love to her in the shower and then his bed. Over and over. Somehow his cock kept rising as if it knew this was all the time left with her.

In the wee hours of the night, she'd finally given him the words he'd wanted to hear: "I love you, Virgil." She fell asleep curled against him, a warm, fragrant, soft—obstinately independent—woman.

He watched, heart aching. Surely he could figure out a way to make this work.

Chapter Twelve

MORNING SUNLIGHT STREAMING through the window and across the quilt awakened Summer. She blinked and frowned. The quilt was the wrong color. *Not my bed.* But the pillow held an appealing scent of mountain and man. And the whole room smelled of sex. Virgil's room. She wiggled in pleasure and winced at her aching inner thigh muscles, sore nipples and pussy.

Her butt definitely felt abused.

Why did the memory of him taking her there, somewhere so private—so forbidden—make her want to beg for his use again? *Who have I turned into?* Something at her core trembled. He'd controlled her last night. Completely. Physically and emotionally. In the bed, holding her hands over her head, deep inside her, demanding that she tell him how she felt. Rumbling his satisfaction when she'd gasped out, "I love you, Virgil." He'd made her scream it again as she came.

He'd held her so sweetly she wanted to be back in his arms. Forever.

The ache of loss threatened to grow, and she sat up. The room was empty. "Virgil?"

Shoving her tangled hair out of her face, she looked around. A nice comfy bedroom with no clutter. More cream-colored walls, heavy, dark wood dresser and tables, rich brown carpeting. The colors matched those of his mountain, she realized. He had a store-bought quilt in deep greens and blues. *Maybe I should make him a real one.*

On the bedside stand, she spotted a note:

Slugger

She grinned and glanced at her bruised knuckles.

Got called in to work—hopefully will be back this morning. I left some clothes on a chair for you. Coffee is in kitchen downstairs. Use the door in the corner of the bedroom. Make yourself at home.

Love you, V

Oh God. She tried to quell the warmth engulfing her. "*Love you.*" How easily he used the L word. She sighed. Thank God he snored, or she might think he was perfect.

After her shower, she found clothes on the bedroom chair. One faded pair of jeans fit despite being tight in the butt. She donned a T-shirt, then pulled on a huge flannel shirt. It had to be Virgil's. She rolled the sleeves up and felt engulfed in softness.

Must have caffeine. With single-minded need, she headed downstairs, through a rustic living room big as her apartment, and into an oversize country kitchen with brick-colored walls.

Coffeemaker, check. Coffee, check.

As the magnificent scent of brewing coffee filled the room, she considered the coming day. She had a dreary drive to get back to San Francisco, then an orgy of packing and moving. Funny how her sense of anticipation at starting a new job had diminished so much—because Virgil wouldn't be there. The feeling of loss made an uncomfortable lump in her chest. She shook her head. *Reality check, Summer.* No work, can't stay.

Boots thumped on the stairs, and Summer glanced up. *He's back.* Happy excitement tingled along her nerves. Only…that sounded like more than one pair of footsteps.

"Thank fuck Virg made coffee. I might—" A man stepped into

the kitchen and halted at the sight of her. Another man thumped into him. Both had shaggy brown hair, leathery tans, flannel shirts, and jeans. Big guys.

Oh hell. A thin trickle of fear slid through her. She rose and took a step back. "Um. I—"

"Hey, you must be Summer." The man in the door stepped forward, holding out a hand. "I talked to you on the phone. I'm Wyatt, Virg's brother."

Virgil had brothers? He'd never mentioned anyone except a cousin. *Well, I didn't ask him about his family, now did I?* She winced. No, she'd spent the time talking about herself. *Pitiful, Summer. How self-centered can you get?*

His brothers. Her hair still hung in wet tangles from the shower; she wore Virgil's shirt, and had obviously spent the night. Heat flamed her cheeks. Of course, it could be worse—she could be sitting here in fetishwear.

The two men looked like Virgil. Open rugged faces. Friendly. She shook Wyatt's hand firmly and said, "It's nice to meet you."

"Morgan." The leaner one smiled. "He called, said he's stuck in town booking some drunken bikers. We're supposed to feed you. Then if he's not back, I'll run you up to the lodge."

The sense of disappointment dulled the morning even further. She watched Morgan fill mugs with coffee and tried to find her wits. "Do you guys live here too?"

"Yep." Morgan handed her a mug. "Me and Wyatt and Kallie run a wilderness guide business, so there's livestock. Virgil tends the veggie gardens. It's easier to manage everything if we're here on the property."

Wyatt winked at her. "Downstairs is common territory; upstairs we got our own apartments."

So her Virgil lived in a gorgeous area, had a job, a family, a community. Even a garden. She gave a silent sigh of envy. "Sounds wonderful."

"Works pretty good." Wyatt stuck his head in the magnet-covered refrigerator. "What'd you like for breakfast?"

"Nothing. I need to get going." She'd run back to the lodge and pack, then swing into town. Say good-bye. The thought sliced deep, the pain arriving a second later. *Good-bye.*

"You sure?" Morgan frowned. "You look a little peaked. You should eat."

She shook her head. "It's a long drive. Where's the police station?"

"Midway through town. On the left," Morgan said. "Next to the medical clinic, across from the grocery.

"You have a medical clinic?" Laurette needed a prescription for some of the equipment. Summer could stop by there too. And then she had another thought, and her hands tightened on the coffee mug. "I don't suppose they'd need a nurse?"

Wyatt snorted. "Hell no. Doc hates nurses, hasn't had one for a year or so. He hired some college guy."

"Abe's wife worked for him. Ugly divorce," Morgan said. "He drove a couple nurses off after that. Good doctor, but he's got a temper."

Her spirits sank.

AFTER MORGAN HAD dropped her off at the lodge, she'd started to pack, then driven to the tiny town instead. *I want Virgil.* Not that seeing him would solve anything.

She drove slowly down the Main Street. Dammit, why did Bear Flat have to be so pretty? She scowled at the picturesque stores with colorful hanging signs. A nineteenth-century-style boardwalk. All surrounded by breathtaking, snow-covered mountains. She'd have liked living here. "This isn't helping."

After parking in front of the police department, she sat for a minute, trying to contain the pain in her chest. Virgil didn't need to see her in tears. And she saw no point in a drawn-out good-bye.

She couldn't live on someone else's charity. She had an occupation that she loved.

Maybe he'd come and see her. And she could visit him here—after she worked long enough to have some days off.

But why even try to draw it out? He belonged here, and unless they built a hospital in the area, she never would. They had no future.

Throat tight, eyes burning, she pulled open the door to the police station. One uniformed officer sat at a table in the center of the room, another at a desk in the corner. "Is Virgil here?" she asked when they looked over.

"Should return in a bit." He shook his head. "Hopefully he'll be in a better mood by then."

Guilt hit low and deep. It was because of her.

Her thought must have shown, since the cop grinned. "He and the doc got into it. Masterson was royally piss—" He broke off with an embarrassed glance at her. "Very angry at Abe. Could hear them shouting from in here."

The gray-haired cop in the corner barked a laugh. "Never heard Masterson yell like that afore."

"Okay. Well, thanks." Her unhappiness deepened as she stepped back onto the street. She'd bet that Virgil had tried to find her a job. She scowled at the next-door building, where the black window lettering proclaimed: BEAR FLAT MEDICAL CLINIC. Her next stop.

Wonderful. A doctor who hated nurses and made Virgil lose his temper. She'd just give the receptionist the list for Laurette and get the heck out of Dodge.

In the clinic, the small waiting room stood empty. No one sat at the receptionist's desk. Summer tapped her fingers on the desk impatiently.

Noise filtered through the door leading to the exam rooms. Someone vomiting. A man shouting, "Dammit, get over here. I need—" Cursing. Sounded more like an emergency room than a clinic. An ominous amount of blood had splattered across the tile floor.

Well, it appeared Doctor Prima Donna had problems. *Leave?* Summer glanced at the front door, sighed, squirted handwash from the dispenser on her hands, and headed to the back.

One empty room, another, then…chaos.

A woman, dead-white, sat on the floor in a corner, shaking and crying. Across the room, a young man knelt in a pool of vomit. Lovely.

A beefy male lay on the exam table, covered in blood. Something—maybe an axe—had laid his upper chest open right down to the ribs. Probably the gory sight had toppled the woman and, at a guess, the med tech.

Standing over the patient, the gray-haired doctor was cursing—very inventively—and plainly needed another set of hands. *I'd rather kick you. Really hard.* Summer sighed again, tossed her coat on a chair, and grabbed a pair of gloves from a box on the counter. "You got an ambulance called?" she asked as she pulled them on.

His head jerked up. Gray hair, drawn face, sharp blue eyes behind glasses. "About an hour out," he snapped. "I need some help if you could keep from puking and—"

Summer snorted and glanced at his supplies. The pile of four-by-four sponges he'd used for direct pressure was almost gone. Looked like he might need to tie off a spurter too. The cupboards along the wall were well stocked, and she grabbed a dressing set, absorbable sutures, more gauze four-by-fours, and set up a sterile field on the tray table.

The doctor grunted and set to work.

Summer smiled down into the patient's dazed, pain-ridden eyes. "We'll get some of the bleeding stopped. Then I can give you something for pain. Hang in there a little longer."

He managed a nod.

The doc stared at her for a second. Then his attention returned to the wound. She silently assisted. Once the doc had gotten the bleeding under adequate control, he irrigated, then worked on packing the wound.

With a bare minimum of talk, Summer started an IV and gave the patient some morphine, pleased when the lines of pain on his face eased. She tucked blankets around him, reassured the woman whose color was returning, and set the med tech to cleaning up his mess and the blood.

She ignored the doctor whenever possible. Truly competent, she'd noticed, and surprisingly sweet with the patient—now that he wasn't cursing—but the narrow-minded jerk didn't hire nurses, and he'd made Virgil mad enough to yell. She still wanted to kick him.

After the ambulance crew finally arrived and took the patient away, Summer washed her hands and turned to see the doctor watching her.

"You're the nurse Virgil told me about," he muttered. "I don't like nurses."

God, why did she ever choose a career where she had to deal with doctors? "So I've heard," she said, cold but polite. Fighting never accomplished anything...although right now, it sure sounded tempting. "I brought in a list of things Ms. Laurette needs. Virgil will see to the installation, but some equipment requires a prescription for Medicare to cover it." She dug in her pocket and set the paper on the counter. Two points to her for not throwing it at him.

His scowl deepened. "You're a hospital nurse. What do you know about home medical equipment?"

"I worked closely with the discharge planner." She picked up her coat.

"Hold up," he barked.

She glanced at her watch. She needed to find Virgil, wherever the heck he'd gone, and get her butt on the road. "You're welcome." She pulled open the door of the exam room.

He slapped the door shut. "Jesus, you're as stubborn as Masterson."

Yeah, look who's talking. She folded her hands in front of her and assumed an I'm-being-extremely-patient expression.

He blinked as if in disbelief, then said, "I haven't had good luck with nurses. After my... Well, after one nurse didn't work out, I went through two more." He eyed her, then removed his hand from the door. "One handled the patients well, but she had the judgment of a stump, and the other bawled like a baby every time I snapped at her."

He frowned at the med tech, who still looked green. "I thought I might train someone, but maybe not."

Well, at least the guy could admit he made a mistake. Good for him. Nonetheless, she was running late. She gave him another long-suffering look.

To her surprise, he barked a laugh. "No wonder you impressed Masterson."

When she edged toward the door, he wedged his foot against it and continued talking. "You're experienced, coolheaded, and excellent with people." He glanced at the paper on the counter where she'd listed the equipment she recommended and had starred the ones needing prescriptions. "You're organized."

He crossed his arms over his chest. "Want a job?"

FROM THE PORCH swing of the lodge, Virgil waited as Summer parked her car and stepped out. Smiling a little, she arched her back and stretched, as if reaching for the sky.

Fucking-A, the woman simply took his breath away—like after a winter storm, when sunlight would spill onto the untouched white of the mountains, casting the world into brilliance. And all a man could do was thank God for the gift of that moment.

He leaned forward, elbows on knees, and watched her cross the clearing. When she spotted him, joy lit her eyes. *Thanks, God.*

"Virgil!" Her pace quickened.

Just the sound of her voice made him smile. Made him harden.

Made him hurt to think she'd leave.

But he'd go with her. As she trotted up the steps, his resolve firmed. *I can't give her up.* He'd find a job in her town up north. He could live without the Sierras.

"Logan said you hadn't checked out, so I waited here." Virgil rose and pulled her against him, rubbing his cheek in her hair. She responded as she always did, softening in his arms. Offering herself. Sexiest woman he'd ever known.

"You jerk. I went nuts trying to find you." When she frowned up at him, he captured her lips for a long, gratifying kiss. He slid his hands down, discovering that the jeans he'd loaned her were well past skintight. With a hum of pleasure, he curved his fingers under her round ass and murmured, "Be very polite right now, sweetheart. After last night, you're too tender to fuck senseless."

Pink flooded her cheeks, and then she wiggled her hips. "I'm not that sore." Mischief turned her eyes sky blue.

His cock responded as if she'd raised the starting gate, and he almost groaned. Dammit. Now he'd suffer with a massive hard-on while they loaded her car.

She grinned at him, tilting her hips against his dick.

Hell with it, they'd just get a later start. Before he could scoop her up, she stepped back. "I'd... I want to talk first."

Fucking-A, he might have a stroke right then and there. Good thing she was a nurse. He pulled in a slow breath. "All right."

SUMMER HAD FELT his erection, seen the heat in his gaze. Now she heard the strained patience in his voice. How many men would back off without making a production of it? God, she loved him.

He pulled her down to sit beside him on the porch swing. After putting an arm over her shoulders, he picked up a strand of her hair, curling it around his hand. He really did like to touch. It seemed strange that someone the size of a truck could be so affectionate. She glanced up.

The corners of his eyes crinkled, and he touched her cheek

lightly with his finger. "I love you."

Oh God. In the clear mountain light, his eyes were golden and filled with such warmth that it was like a force pulling her toward him. Dammit, she'd wanted to have a rational discussion. One not involving emotions. "Virgil…"

"Say it, slugger." He was as unstoppable as spring back home—melting the snow, exposing the tender new grass, flooding the streams and tearing away obstacles. Pushing her off-balance.

"I love you too." And she did, and her feelings for him kept growing, sending out leaves, rooting deep in her soul. She blinked back tears. "I love you so much."

"There we go." He kissed her gently, then said, "I took the week off. I'm going to help you move and get settled in…if that doesn't frighten you too much. I can do a little job-hunting myself." He ran his finger down her cheek, smiling at her startled look. "I daresay I can find work somewhere close to you."

"I'm staying."

"But we'd best get started and…" He started to rise, then froze. "Wait… What did you say?"

Bubbles of joy rising inside her were as heady as champagne, and she giggled, then gave him a stern look and repeated his own words back to him, "Oh, you heard me."

When he still just stared at her, she wrapped an arm around his neck, pulling him down to whisper, "I'll stay."

"Thank you, God." His arms tightened until her ribs creaked, and then he kissed the breath right out of her. He was going to kill her dead—and she wouldn't want to be anywhere else in the world.

He cupped her head, holding her against him for a moment, and she heard his heart pounding under her ear. "What about your career?" he finally asked.

"The doctor in town hired me."

"Well damn." He pushed her back to stare into her face in disbelief. "How the hell did you do that? I—uh—"

"Yeah, I know you yelled at him." She touched his hard jaw with fingers that trembled slightly. He'd lost his temper, not at her but to help her. How could she not love him? "So I'm staying. But…I'm going to get my own place."

His eyes narrowed ominously. "You won't move in with me?"

"No." *Firm. Be firm, Summer.* "It's too soon. We need to see how it goes. So I'll get an apartment or—"

"Not an apartment. Hell, I almost forgot." He rose and strode into the lodge in big ground-covering strides.

She stared after him.

A minute later, he returned, a small quilt bundled in his arms.

She frowned. "You wanted a blanket?"

"Didn't want him to get cold," he muttered and opened the quilt to drop something in her lap. Something that squirmed with soft, soft fur, long drooping ears, big brown eyes.

The spaniel puppy bounced up to frantically lick her chin, wiggling in joy.

"Oh, look at you… You're so cute." Laughing, Summer glanced up at Virgil. "You got a puppy?"

"Nope. *You* got a puppy." He smiled at her, and the love in his eyes filled her heart to overflowing. "I planned to come with you, but if you refused and left without me"—his jaw tightened as he repeated—"if you left alone, you'd be hurting almost as much as me, and you'd need something to love."

As he took his seat beside her, she buried her face in the puppy's soft fur, trying not to cry. He'd have tried to make her happy even if she left him. How could her heart keep expanding without bursting? Still holding the squirmy puppy, she stood and plopped down on Virgil's lap.

He rumbled a laugh, and his arms came around her and the pup, offering a warm shelter of protection. Here was everything she ever wanted.

He'd said, "*I learned a harsh lesson this year that I should never assume someone knows how I feel.*" That applied to her too. "I love you, Virgil."

"Now that's exactly what I wanted to hear," he said softly. He cupped her cheek. "I will always do my best to fill your needs." It sounded like a vow. The sun lines at the corners of his eyes crinkled, and his voice deepened with controlled power. "Since it appears I'm a fucking pervert…a *dom*"—his smile flickered—"that means you will fill all of mine."

At the undeniable command, a wave of heat surged over her, melting every single bone. He lifted an eyebrow, waiting for her answer.

"Yes, Sir," she whispered. Then she raised her chin. "But I'm still going to have my own place. At least six months." Surely she could hold out for that long, just to make sure they really were suited.

As he studied her face, she realized he was reading her like an open book…and he'd only been a dom a little while. The memory of last night came to her—his powerful hands and hard voice controlling her. A tremor ran through her. What would happen as he grew more experienced? She lifted her gaze.

Watchful intelligence burned in his level eyes…and then he gave her a slow, utterly confident smile.

Oh God, she'd be lucky to last a month.

~ *The End* ~

Reviews

I adore getting reviews for my books. And as a reader, I rely on y'all's opinions to help me decide which story I should buy next. So…if you get a chance, I'd love if you left a review for *Master of the Dark Side*.

Mountain Masters & Dark Haven: 5

My Liege of Dark Haven

MY LIEGE OF DARK HAVEN exceeded my expectations. It takes a lot of talent and hard work to maintain such high consistency in a series but Cherise Sinclair seems to hit it right every time. It's no wonder why she's at the very top of my auto buy list for this genre! Simply put, Sinclair will thrill and excite you. Master Xavier is so hot, he'll leave you breathing fire!

~ Under the Covers Reviews

Threatened by university cutbacks, Professor Abigail Bern's only hope is to publish a provocative research paper—soon. Planning to covertly observe behavior in the notorious Dark Haven BDSM club, she takes a receptionist job. When the owner calls upon her to assist in a demonstration, she's appalled. Then fascinated. Under the unyielding hands of the master known as *my Liege*, she discovers a need to be more than an observer.

His late wife had been the center of his life, and Xavier Leduc wants no other. But when his new receptionist does her utmost to keep an emotional distance from him, he's intrigued and digs deeper. She's adorable. Intriguingly intelligent, beautifully submissive, sweetly vulnerable. He soon realizes her defenses are keeping her on the fringe of her sexuality—and her life. As he draws her into fuller participation, she unconsciously does the same for him. She begins to fill his world.

Ever since the night she met my Liege Xavier, Abby has questioned everything she believes about herself. She's falling for the stern owner of Dark Haven and thinks he's beginning to care for her…until the day he learns why she's in his club.

Excerpt from

My Liege of Dark Haven

"**A**BBY, SINCE WE'VE not played together before, you tell me if something is getting to be too much."

It's already too much. Abby looked over her shoulder at the owner of the club. White dress shirt, black silk vest, black jeans, black boots. Definitely in the tall, dark, and handsome category, only the words seemed insipid compared to the reality. The wide muscular shoulders turned *tall* into dangerous. His skin held the darkness of Native American ancestry, and the long black braid down his back was a definite statement. Very handsome, with European chiseled features that went well into hard-edged.

And scary. But she couldn't back out. She doubted the man had a benevolent bone in his body. Quite obviously if she didn't "assist," she'd be out the door. She sure hadn't thought her participant observations would include *real* participation. Unease tickled the back of her throat.

He glanced up, and the sun lines at the corners of his eyes crinkled with amusement. "Easy, Abby. The club safe word is *red*, and if you use it, play stops immediately. Say it loudly, and a dungeon monitor will show up to make sure you're all right." Holding her arm firmly, he wrapped what looked like wide packing tape around her right wrist a couple of times, and she realized the material wasn't sticky.

"Red. Got it."

"Abby," he said. "I daresay you know how to address a Dominant in this setting, especially the one working with you."

The uninflected reprimand made her flush as if she'd been caught cheating off someone's test paper. "Yes, my liege."

He didn't rant but nodded acceptance.

Despite her relief that he hadn't lost his temper, anxiety thrummed in her ears as he pulled her other arm behind her back and secured both wrists together. She closed her eyes and tried to pretend nothing was happening. She'd never been able to let Nathan put her in handcuffs. Why in the world was she allowing this stranger to restrain her arms?

But she needed this place for her fieldwork. Needed to keep her job. *Publish or perish.* If she ever met the academic who'd invented that phrase, she'd shove his papers down his throat until he choked.

"Abby."

She opened her eyes.

Xavier stood in front of her, looking down. Why did he have to be so tall? His warm hands massaged her bare shoulders. "Any strain in your joints?"

"No, sir."

He studied her silently.

She shifted her weight, trying not to think about her lack of mobility. If she didn't move, she wouldn't know—much like closing her eyes during gory movie scenes.

"Pull on the tape, Abby. How does it feel?"

Her arms jerked involuntarily, and just like that she knew she was restrained. Couldn't defend herself. That her body was available to the impassive-faced Master. Alternating waves of heat and cold rushed over her as if she stood in front of a rotating fan. She pulled harder, and panic squeezed her throat.

"Easy, pet." He cupped her chin with one firm hand. His fingers curled around her arm, creating a warm place on her skin. His movements showed how easily he could touch her…yet the contact was comforting. Settling. "Eyes on me."

Panting, she looked up and into eyes the color of darkness, but the specks of golden brown made them warm, not cold.

"Good girl. You know you can't escape, but I'm not going to do anything you won't enjoy. We're here in a public place, and you have a safe word that will summon every monitor in the dungeon. Now slow your breathing down before you hyperventilate."

Oops. His gaze never left hers as she pulled in a measured breath and let it out.

"Better. Another." His grip on her upper arm was unyielding but not painful. A man's hand.

Why did his touch seem different from Nathan's? Why didn't she get that horrible dread?

"Little fluff, I want you to remember how you're breathing now. When I tighten a clamp, it will hurt for a few seconds. I want you to inhale through the pain like you did with your fear."

"Pain? But—"

"Do you get flu shots?"

"Yes." When his eyebrows pulled together, she added a hasty, "My liege."

"This is the same level of pain, although people rarely get turned on by vaccinations. Whereas nipple clamps..." A crease appeared and disappeared in his cheek.

She nodded to say she could handle that much pain. But could she handle these disconcerting flares of heat? Her nipples actually tingled as if anticipating the touch of those powerful fingers.

Was this the kind of thing Nathan had wanted to do with her? Guilt pressed on her chest. Considering he had dumped her, she shouldn't feel as if she were betraying him. But she did. And she'd let a complete stranger restrain her. Alice had fallen down a hole into Wonderland; Abby had fallen into quicksand and was sinking fast. *What am I doing here?*

Xavier hadn't moved, was simply watching her. "What's the matter, Abby?"

"I don't know you at all. You're talking about..." *Nipple clamps.* "I don't *know* you."

"I see." His hand was still curved around her upper arm as he moved closer. With his fingers under her chin, he lifted her face and gave her a light kiss. His lips were firm but velvety. Gentle. How could someone with such a merciless face kiss so sweetly?

When he lifted his head, she whispered, "Why did you do that?"

His aftershave was totally masculine with a hint of the exotic, like a pirate who'd visited India. He rubbed his thumb in a circle over her cheek, his lips only an inch from hers. "Because I can," he whispered back. Then he smiled. "Because I'm going to be touching you much more intimately in a moment."

Heat roared through her at the thought of his hands...elsewhere.

"Think of this as an introduction. I'm Xavier." He covered her mouth with his, and it wasn't a gentle, sweet kiss any longer. He took her lips, demanding a response. When she pulled at the restraints and gasped, his tongue swept in. She couldn't move, couldn't escape, and...

He stepped back, grasping her arms to keep her steady. Ravished by only a kiss, she stared at him. Her lips felt swollen, and she ran her tongue over them.

A flicker of heat lit his eyes, followed by amusement. "Are we better acquainted now?"

Her voice came out sounding as if he'd strangled her instead of kissing her. "Yes, my liege." If he introduced himself like that at a faculty party, the floor would be littered with swooning academics.

"Very good." With far-too-competent hands, he undid the first hook on her corset. As he worked his way down, his long fingers slid between her full breasts, brushing the insides. Each undone fastening exposed more of her body, and coolness wafted over her damp flesh. When he finished, he set the corset to one side, leaving her bare from the waist up.

She bit her lip. *Really, this is nothing.* In France, beaches were filled with women wearing no tops. Not that she had joined them, but… She took a mental step back. *Observe.* With a determined breath, she checked out a noisy spanking in the center of the room.

A warm hand cupped her breast.

She jumped, tried to pull away. "What are you doing?"

He grasped her arm with his other hand, holding her in place. "Did you think you could get clamps without being touched by the Dom?" Even as he spoke, he stroked her breasts, one then the other. His palm was calloused, slightly abrasive. His thumb circled the areola, and her nipple bunched hard enough to create an ache.

She tried to dissociate, to observe the other scene.

"Eyes on me, Abby." The softness of his voice didn't negate the command.

Also from Cherise Sinclair

Masters of the Shadowlands (contemporary)
Club Shadowlands
Dark Citadel
Breaking Free
Lean on Me
Make Me, Sir
To Command and Collar
This Is Who I Am
If Only
Show Me, Baby
Servicing the Target

Mountain Masters and Dark Haven (contemporary)
Master of the Mountain
Simon Says: Mine (novella)
Master of the Abyss
Master of the Dark Side (novella)
My Liege of Dark Haven
Edge of the Enforcer
Master of Freedom

The Wild Hunt Legacy (paranormal)
Hour of the Lion
Winter of the Wolf

Standalone books
The Starlight Rite (Sci-Fi Romance)
The Dom's Dungeon (contemporary)

About Cherise Sinclair

Authors often say their characters argue with them. Unfortunately, since Cherise Sinclair's heroes are Doms, she never, ever wins.

A *USA Today* Bestselling Author, she's renowned for writing heart-wrenching romances with devastating Dominants, laugh-out-loud dialogue, and absolutely sizzling sex. And did I mention the BDSM? Her numerous awards include a National Leather Award, *Romantic Times* Reviewer's Choice nomination, and Best Author of the Year from the Goodreads BDSM group.

Fledglings having flown the nest, Cherise, her beloved husband, and one fussy feline live in the Pacific Northwest where nothing is cozier than a rainy day spent writing.

Connect with Cherise in the following places:

Website:
http://CheriseSinclair.com

Facebook:
www.facebook.com/CheriseSinclairAuthor

Facebook Discussion Group:
CheriseSinclair.com/Facebook-Discussion-Group

Want to be notified of the next release?

Sent only on release day, Cherise's newsletters contain freebies, excerpts, and articles.
Sign up at:
www.CheriseSinclair.com/NewsletterForm